Trying to Be

Trying to Be

John Haskell

FC2

TUSCALOOSA

FC2 is an imprint of the University of Alabama Press
Inquiries about reproducing material from this work should be addressed to the University of Alabama Press

Book Design: Publications Unit, Department of English, Illinois State University; Director: Steve Halle, Production Interns: Addilyn Glass, Sophia Hardy, Reid Karsen, Jacob Lyle, Molly Oldenburg, Ellie Van Tassel
Cover image: Photograph by Peter Moore; copyright Northwestern University, courtesy of Peter Moore Photography Archive, Charles Deering McCormick Library of Special Collections, Northwestern University Libraries
Cover design: Matthew Revert
Typeface: Adobe Jenson Pro and Helvetica Neue

Cataloging-in-Publication data is available from the Library of Congress.
ISBN: 978-1-57366-214-7
E-ISBN: 978-1-57366-917-7

Contents

Bacon / Velasquez

1

Francis Bacon
the painter was born in Dublin, in 1909, to an heiress mother, and
according to stories his father, an Australian racehorse trainer, was
very strict. And terrifying to young Francis. His paintings, with
their contorted faces gasping for air, reflect that terror—or seem
to—the terror of being unable to take a breath of air because there
is no air. There was Bacon, asthmatic, gay at a time when homo-
sexuality was illegal in England, and one of the people he painted
was his lover, George Dyer. They met, the story goes, when Dyer,
a petty criminal from the East End of London, broke into Bacon's
apartment and Bacon, seeing this affable young ruffian ransack-
ing his house, became enamored. First intrigued, then enamored,
and you can say that opposites attract but these two were more
like twins, like mirror images, like Romulus and the other one, the
brother he killed. Although Dyer was twenty-four years younger
than Bacon, looking at photographs, the two men have the same
square faces, the same pomaded hair, the same taste for rough sex
and hard drinking but Bacon also had ambition, which pulled him
away from Dyer, into a circle of sophistication and money that was
foreign to Dyer, like a foreign language, and like the bridge that initially connected them, after a while, the cables of that bridge began
to fray. Dyer's dependence and drunkenness began to get on Bacon's nerves, and he turned his attention more and more away from
Dyer, to people who'd achieved the fame he coveted, artists like
Velazquez and Picasso and Dyer, I imagine, felt left out. Out of his

depth, as he probably never said, but Bacon helped him financially. Even after they'd broken up, he invited him to Paris to celebrate his retrospective at the Grand Palais. This was a big deal, and possibly he wanted Dyer, who knew what he'd *been*, to see what he'd *become*, to witness the adoration that must have left Dyer, standing alone at the bar, feeling superfluous. How could it not? These images on the walls, he said, that's me, my body, my naked body as I stood or sat or contorted myself like that, bent like that, hour after hour and now my *actual* body has been discarded. That's what it feels like. And maybe some people find that kind of debasement arousing, a turn-on, but I don't, Dyer said, or I didn't. I'm dizzy, that's what I'm trying to say. My head is spinning. My skin is clammy and damp, and my heart is beating faster than normal, faster than it ought to, and even worse than the feeling of vertigo is the moment when the vertigo, like a mist, like a cushion made of mist, evaporates. That's when I wander out onto the streets of Paris, cruising the dampened avenues, the foggy boulevards of broken expectations, stumbling, drunk, with a bottle in one hand and an eager young acquaintance holding the other, inviting himself to my room, to Bacon's room, the room in which, later, slumped on the toilet, sitting but not quite sitting, as if balancing on a cushion of porcelain, I would be found, dead.

2

Diego Velazquez
was a painter who painted the people who could afford his services, queens and kings, and they didn't call it a lifestyle in 1600 but Velasquez probably had one, hobnobbing with the rich and famous, being only slightly *less* rich and *less* famous, and *paint what you know*, that's what they say, and that's why the people in his paintings, some of them, seem worried, as if they'd been caught,

again, having done something wrong, and the sense of culpability is palpable, pestering them like a memory, like an insect buzzing around your ear. If all his portraits were lined up against a wall they'd all look basically like what they are, realistic representations of particular people. But if you let your eyes relax, wandering across the canvas surfaces, wandering into the eyes of one of his painted faces—and you only need one, take your pick—you can start to see the mental and physical and emotional contortion necessary to portray, in every sitter who sat in front of him, himself. In 1650, on a trip to Italy, he was commissioned to paint a portrait of the pope, Innocent X. In those days popes were hardly innocent, and Innocent was probably vain, certainly powerful, and the painting shows him looking out toward the camera, regarding the camera which of course wasn't a camera but the eyes of Velasquez, who'd painted jesters and drunkards, and because every painting, so they say, is a form of self-portraiture, Innocent comes off, not only as a pious, devoted seeker after truth, but also as a businessman, canny and skeptical, someone who, over the years, might have been a little careless, a little cavalier, not unscrupulous exactly but now he believes that someone is mad at him, or after him, and being a pope, someone probably was. In the painting he tries to camouflage his anxiety but you can see, in the face Velasquez painted, in the eyes and brow and jaw, his self-reproach. And because the likeness wasn't necessarily flattering, some of the pope's assistants worried. Would the pontiff like the likeness? Or would he find it insulting and demeaning? And would his displeasure at how Velasquez had represented him on the canvas translate into anger and repudiation and recrimination? According to reports, when the old pope saw the image of himself created by Velasquez he simply said, *È troppo vero.* It's too true.

3

I can almost imagine

what it might possibly have felt like, for Bacon, after the champagne and the adulation at the Grand Palais, walking down the carpeted hotel hallway, back to the room where you knock on the door and it's fine when Dyer doesn't answer. He's been drinking, as have you, so no problem. So you keep knocking. But then you remember that you have the key in your pocket. You've had it all along. And whether it's too true, or whether it really happened, you use the key to open the door, and George? You have a pet name for him. You say it. Is it *Lucky?* You whisper it, and the smell when you enter the room, with the bed still unmade, the sheets twisted up like the rope Rapunzel used when she lowered herself from the tow-er, doesn't seem very lucky. Lacquered, plastered, hammered. He's been drinking and crying, probably puking his guts out, pitting his pain against yours, wanting his to be bigger than yours, more ur-gent than yours. Or mine. And because he's your friend, you wait a very long time but he doesn't appear. He doesn't emerge from the bathroom, stumbling and apologetically. And your friendship obliges you to play the game he likes to play, hide and seek, olly olly oxen, we used to say. Free, we used to say, but this time, even be-fore you walk to where he is, even before you find his body, you've seen the scene you're going to paint. In the middle of it, framed by the bathroom door, a man is melting, dissolving into the toilet and into the floor, and melting into himself, his damp skin dusted as if with confectioner's sugar. His underwear is soiled, his belly more distended than you remember. The whiskey bottle is right there where he dropped it, almost empty. And you feel a *ccri de coeur* but you can't be sure if it's him crying out, or it's you, the electrical current entering *you,* and *cri de coeur* is what the French call a feel-ing that doesn't quite disappear, that doesn't dissipate or evaporate, and the black flies swirling around your head are larger than flies, more like wasps, or hornets, and the Greeks had a name for what they were, Furies. Aeschylus, the so-called father of tragedy, wrote a play in which they follow the hero, Orestes, like a plague. The interns from the gallery, when they find you, take you by the arm and gently herd you away from the scene, back to your room and your bed, and it doesn't matter if you're hallucinating. The bees you hear are like bees in the old cartoon, the one where the bear, in an effort to steal the honey, swipes at the hive and out they swarm to protect themselves, to right the wrong that's been done to them, and even when they get you out of your clothes and under the sheets and turn off the lights, you can't stop seeing your old, dead friend.

4

A few years ago
I had a friend who resembled me, so people said. We had roughly the same height, same coloring, same gangly way of walking, and we didn't think exactly alike but we thought about the same *kinds* of things. He was older, more successful, but that wasn't a problem until, at one point, he was planning to visit me, to stay for a day or two at my house. I was distracted, careless, thinking about a trip I was taking that August, to Italy. And what I did must have been unforgivable because our friendship, which had seemed to be stable and solid, disintegrated. We broke up. He stopped speaking to me, stopped writing to me, and all I could do was accept, as fact, my banishment. It was over, our affair, and what's been surprising to me is that not a week goes by, or sometimes it's more like a month, or two, when I don't have a dream in which my friend plays a starring role. Haunts my dreams is more what he does, and in the beginning I hated it. This person had cut me out of his life, had found such fault in me as merited repudiation, and why would I want to dream about that, about being hurt? And I *was* hurt. He'd

been able to abandon me so easily. I didn't want to be the kind of person who cared about misunderstandings. The past, I wanted to think, is over. I wanted to believe that whatever mistakes I've made, *if* I've made them, now it's time to move on. But the dreams kept recurring, dreams in which my friend would be standing in a line, in front of me or behind me, waiting to pick up his tickets or his keys, and in the early dreams I didn't even speak to him. Sometimes he'd be sitting on a stage, or having a drink at a bar. Often he'd brought along a friend, usually someone intelligent, more intelligent than me, seemingly, and more adept at the ins and outs of whatever business we were all involved in. Sometimes it was hiking. If I had escaped into nature, to an area just above the tree line, to walk across the wildflower meadows with nothing but sky and rocks and birdsongs in the trees, he would appear, out of the blue, usually walking in the opposite direction. Usually with a group of admirers. And he would be civil to me in the dream, which made it worse. He could afford to be civil because, in his mind, I was the one who had wronged him, and maybe I had, and the price I paid was that I didn't matter to him. And I didn't. And I wanted to feel for him a compensatory nonchalance. I wanted to stop needing and hating and dreaming of him, measuring my life against his life, and losing. And I do lose. And I say I don't mind and I want *not* to mind but I can't stop feeling this loathing, which probably ought to be called what it is, self-loathing, because it's directed at me.

5

Starting in the 1950s
Bacon began painting variations on the Velazquez portrait of Pope Innocent. They're all different, but they all express . . . It's hard to say what exactly the paintings express. Pain, dread, fear, guilt, the anxiety of being in a human body. In one variation, *Study after*

Velazquez's Portrait of Pope Innocent X, the pope is wearing a purple vestment, sitting on a glowing golden chair that looks like an electric chair. *Feels*, I should say, as if an electric current is pulsing up through the chair and into the pope who's caught, mid-gesture, mouth agape, obscured by a veil of quasi-electric striations that seem to cage him or confine him, and the surge he feels is less a shock and more like a steady continuous agony. The body, distorted by that agony, is crying out, and Bacon either feels it or intuits it, and even if every now and then it seems about to lift, like a mist, it returns, following him and gnawing at him, and his painted renditions of Innocent are constantly changing what Innocent is, or was, preserving roughly the facts of the scene but trying to change the emotions you don't want to feel until, eventually, maybe they go away.

6

Las Meninas
is a large painting by Diego Velasquez in which a princess, the only child of the king and queen of Spain, prepares herself to . . . I don't know what she's preparing to do but she occupies the middle of the canvas, her two meninas flanking her, along with dwarves and a dog, and a mirror is barely visible at the back of the painting. In it, they say, is the likeness of the king and queen. And if you think about it geometrically, if they're in a mirror and we're looking at their faces, then they must be standing right about where we are. And if the mirror actually *is* a mirror and not a painting of one then we see *our* faces where *their* faces are. Pablo Picasso, a hundred years later, re-created his own variations of *Las Meninas*. The Velasquez must have reminded him of something he'd seen, or done, or not done. And whatever it was, he couldn't get it out of his head. So he painted it. He changed the characters,

their personalities and relationships, and one variation from 1957 is black and white, blue and white really, washed out, more like a drawing, a painted drawing. In the center he's put the Infanta, her iconic hoop dress with its gigantic bustle rising out of her backside. In the mirror, where Velazquez had placed the king and queen, now there's just one face, half smiling like a happy emoji face but not completely happy. In the original, where two meninas offer the princess a small red cup of tea, in Picasso's version it looks like they're handing off the swaddled body of a child, a baby, and the figure in the far doorway walking up a flight of stairs, instead of a chamberlain or counsellor or mentor, is the wingèd incarnation of death, that's how I read it, both angel and devil, and holding what must be a brush, the painter stands behind his easel, vibrating with color, facing a canvas that we can't see, one eye regarding his work of art, one eye regarding us, and one eye looking at themselves; and I say *themselves* because it seems as if multiple personalities must be required to undertake the job of re-creating an event that, although it happened three hundred years ago, is still happening.

7

Even after Dyer died
Bacon kept painting his likenesses. A triptych from the early 1970s shows the scene of Dyer's death with Dyer, in the left panel, shitting, his pants around his ankles. In the right panel he's vomiting into a sink. The center panel shows a naked lightbulb over his head becoming a bird or a bat and below his twisted body a dark shape is swallowing him, that's how it seems to me, not a devil exactly but with wings like a bat or a devil, and it could be an angel but now it's too late. *Paint what you know.* And if I don't know how to paint then there's nothing to do except speak, or scream, like cicadas or crickets or butterflies, like Dyer's dying breath, painted over

and over onto the canvas, into an image that becomes a container to hold what would otherwise devour you, furious and persistent, gnawing at you like the Furies gnawing at me, with a purpose, to punish. And sometimes I'm sorry for the things that I've done, and sometimes I even admit it. Sometimes I think I deserve, or I want, to be flogged with a jet-black riding crop, slapped with a pair of brown leather gloves, my swollen face pressed against a plaster wall, hands behind my back, pinned, my lips cutting into my teeth, staining the wall with my blood and spit and Bacon had lovers, usually older, like his father, but then came George. And then George died. And now the swarming is almost audible, a buzzing light bulb about to explode. And it's not that I can't live with myself. Whatever cross I have to bear, I can bear it. Except it's not a cross. It's the air I breathe and it's filled with . . . What to call it? A flock? A crowing? A *frenzy*, that's the word. An individual grasshopper is harmless enough but when they get together a frenzy ensues, transforming their carelessness into wantonness, their wantonness into destruction, hopping from plant to plant, consuming what they can, everything they can, and the ones in the ancient tragedy, eventually, are appeased by the gods, but the ones that circle my head won't leave me.

Peter Moore, *Trisha Brown's Man Walking Down the Side of a Building, 80 Wooster St., New York*, 1970.

Blow Me Away

At the end of the last century an orator named F. M. Alexander codified a way of understanding, or at least thinking about, the body. It's called the Alexander Technique, and it's about aligning the body, or *realigning it*, taking it apart and thinking about how it might fit back together. The problem he found with the body was the way we imagine it. Or really the way we *fail* to imagine it, letting our bodies adapt to habits we don't even know we have. We tell our bodies to disregard imbalance. If there's pain, we say *ignore it, turn away*, which leads to what Alexander called *debauched kinesthetics*, or *erroneous perception*, the idea that we have certain sensations—the information we get from the eyes, nose, muscles, et cetera—and then there's perception, what the mind does with those sensations. Let's say that when I stand, with my feet on the ground and my eyes facing forward, the right side of my body is slightly shorter than the left, as if I'm holding a weighted bag in my hand and the weight of the bag is pulling me down, curving me over. Instead of standing with the verticality of a plumb line, there's a slight arc to my torso. And however I came to this posture, via trauma or repetition or necessity, over time I've made it my history. It's how I perceive who I am, and the longer I live like this, holding the imaginary weight, the more the curve gets embedded in my flesh, memorized by the fibers of my mind and muscle, and more than a habit, it gets like a fact, and it *is* a fact, a fact of my body. The imbalance, caused by the weight, works its way up my arm to the muscles of my shoulder, my scapula pulling my neck, my neck pulling my clavicle, my clavicle pulling my ribs; and eventually my spine has to compensate. As does my mind, normalizing itself by convincing me that I'm standing as straight as an arrow. And even if I release the weight and allow my shoulder girdle to reposition itself, letting my psoas relax and my rib cage realign, although I might be standing verifiably upright, it feels weird. I'd painstakingly built this posture and now, being used to it, even without the weight in my hand, my body keeps holding the *tension* of holding the weight. Which is why Alexander looked at himself in mirrors, to see his body as if from outside, as if from God's eye, as if God had an eye, and he did it because he didn't trust what his body was telling him.

The movie *Blow-Up* was made in 1966, and like any movie, it's partly about the time it was made, about the attitudes and assumptions that existed then, and were normal then, and now it's like a documentary, showing how people used to live, how they stood and walked, and how they tried to be with other people. It begins with two wannabe fashion models knocking on the door of a famous photographer. They're wearing outfits popular at the time, bright sleeveless dresses, hot-pink pantyhose, long bangs, wide eyes, and because it's 1966 they've been reading *Tiger Beat*, watching *Ready, Steady, Go!* And *wannabe* wasn't a word back then but what they *want to be* is clear. They want to be seen. That's why they knock on the door of the photographer, and that's why they audition for him. In the movie he sits in a big leather chair, twirling a coin between his fingers, not really paying attention to them and that's when they notice, behind them, a rack of clothes, the latest styles from Paris and Milan, and suddenly they feel giddy. *Are we allowed to try them on?* Giddy literally means *possessed by a god*, and it's hard to tell if the feeling they have is excitement or anxiety. Or confusion. Or all three. Later, the talkative one will get famous for singing songs in French with a Frenchman, Serge Gainsbourg, but now the younger version of who she's going to become is still learning the ropes. That's what they call the rules of the game, and in 1966 people talked about *changing* the rules, about shedding inhibitions, which is why she unzips her brightly printed dress, lets her shoulder bag fall to the floor, lets her half-naked body be pulled to the room where she tries to follow the photographer's directions, trying to hear what he wants her to do but the music is loud and he seems to want something sexual, for her to *be* sexual. Orgy, the word, meant something different back then, implying not debauchery but liberation, and self-determination, and during the scene he takes out his camera to capture her, posing her in front of a colorful roll of unfurled paper they used to call seamless, a neutral background that had no context but now we can see what the context is. Power. Who has it, who wants it, and who can you trust with your body. I've always felt that *my* body, being distinct from other bodies, separated me from other people, and protected me. My body is here, and other people have other bodies, in other locations, and the idea that bodies can live together is something I'm still getting used to. That's why, watching *Blow-Up*, I identify with the model, Jane Birkin. I see myself, not quite naked, but standing in front of the neutral background and letting myself be photographed, letting myself be told what to do, how to stand, how to be, and later, looking at the photographs, I can see what's happened to my body. My shoulders. They aren't completely level. One side is slightly higher than the other, the one that holds the bag, and the bag is the same bag I've carried my entire life, the one the photographer called diabolical, and although he meant *stylistically*, it makes me think about what a bag like that can do to a person, and did do, to me.

The screenplay for *Blow-Up* was written by Edward Bond. He was an English writer for the theatre and years ago, when I was an actor, I played a part in one of his early plays. *Saved.* It's about a group of young men, a gang, who end up killing a small child, a baby in a pram. The cause is partly accidental but also, according to Bond, aggression is a natural outcome of an unjust society. Violence is a response to the fact that some people have power and privilege, and some people don't. His early plays were famously violent. I was living in London when I saw his play *Lear*. I was staying in Hammersmith, camping out in a derelict factory, and the story is based on Shakespeare, about a king who spends his capital building a wall, what he imagines will be a force for order and goodness. And when it becomes the opposite, he tries to tear it down. But it's too late. And the tragedy of the play is the question left unanswered. How do you tear down what you've painstakingly built? The version I saw was produced by the Royal Shakespeare Company, and the night I saw it, when I got back to my hovel by the river, apparently, while I was gone, thieves had come, ransacked my carefully concealed hiding place, stolen my rucksack and my sleeping bag, and I remember the king in the play, mad with grief, talking to his dead daughter. She'd been lost, and now she was dead, killed for fighting injustice. Her body was lying on a long wooden table, center stage, and from where I sat in the audience I couldn't see the wound they'd made in her belly but I remember the actor playing Lear, like a surgeon, dipping his hands into the middle of her being, into the bowl between her ribcage and her pubic bone, and although it took a few days, that image eventually lodged itself in my body. Since I didn't have a place to stay I spent my time wandering London, stopping at bookstores, and in one of them I found a copy of the text of the play. It was a blue paperback with a photo of Bond on the back cover. I read the play, then read his introduction to the play, then I found his essays about his other plays, and about writing, and socialism, and he seemed to be someone who felt the effects of injustice, who saw how power deforms our social interactions, turns them violent, and instead of running away he pointed it out to the rest of us. My tendency was to turn away, to run from what I didn't like, whatever felt uncomfortable or dangerous, and he seemed to say that running away is fine, if that's what you want, but it isn't necessary. *When you are frighted of the dark you do not* make it go away by shutting your eyes. In his writing about theater, Bond often used the word rational like someone else might use the word fair or just or common sense. It's commonsensical to open our eyes and see that we don't have to hurt each other. That's what I took him to mean, and what I wanted to ask him wasn't rhetorical. I really wanted to know. How do you acknowledge a corrupted history and still have pity on the people who carry that history in our bodies?

Michelangelo Antonioni, still from *Blow-Up*, 1966.

My Ulrike Complex

No one knows exactly how I died. They know I was in a prison. They know I was found with a prison towel tied around my neck. They know I'd been a writer and journalist and, having read Gramsci and Marcuse, when I looked at the world I could see injustice. It ought to have been eradicated long ago. But that's the problem with injustice, it never seems to go away. It feeds on power, clinging to privilege, attaching itself to the people with money, and the people with the money are the same people they've always been. When I was alive I looked at the wars being fought, in Ireland, Vietnam, in Watts; and they were the same old wars they'd always been. *Think of all the hate there is in red China, Then take a look around to Selma, Alabama.* That's from a song, written when I was alive, about leaving earth for *four days in space, but when you return it's the same old place.* It was performed on a television show in 1965, a variety show called *Hullabaloo*, and the lyrics were all about desolation and despair, about the world on the eve of destruction. But on television, because despair didn't sell merchandise, backup dancers danced to the lyrics, writhing on a set meant to look like a junkyard, turning disaffection into another sexy commodity. *Every day, to earn my daily bread I go to the market where lies are traded.* That's from a song by Bertolt Brecht, and maybe because I'd been an orphan, the lies I saw around me, couched in the same old stories, seemed so obvious. I didn't want to buy them, or sell them. I wanted to resist them, or destroy them. And I tried. I left my husband, my children, the magazine I worked for, and as my resistance began to solidify, my beliefs became more radical. I felt more and more the necessity to uproot the story I was taught and start, not from scratch, but by shining light on what was corrupt and unacceptable in that story, maybe you can make it visible, and by making it visible, you can fight it. But it's hard. Because what you're fighting is your own story.

My chance to fight the story I'd been taught came in 1968 when Gudrun asked me to help her. A few years earlier, she and her boy-friend, to protest the Vietnam War, set fire to two Frankfurt department stores. People were hurt, the boyfriend was put in prison, and when she asked me to help she was offering me a chance to turn my good intentions into action, to tear off the so-called *mask of consent*, and I was willing to do it, to turn my back on everything I'd been told was delicious and desirable and change the person I'd spent my life becoming. Sometimes, instead of waiting for the world to change, you need to force it to change, and so I agreed to help Gudrun free her boyfriend, Andreas, from his prison. The plan was simple. Being a journalist, I could easily pose as a journalist writing a story. The prison authorities granted me permission to interview the prisoner, and on the appointed day Andreas was brought to me at the Institute for Social Questions, to the library, wearing handcuffs. The guards assigned to monitor our meeting had guns, so they assumed it was safe to remove his handcuffs. I had my notepad and some cigarettes, and while I was pretending to seriously conduct the interview, three co-conspirators entered the library, placed their briefcases on the polished library tables, and the plan was set in motion. They opened the cases, took out their guns, and as Chekhov says, if you bring a gun to act one, it needs to be shot by the end of the play, and before the end of the interview, or faux interview, shots had been fired, a librarian was hit, and *protest, I once said, is when I say that something doesn't please me. Resistance is when I ensure that what doesn't please me stops happening.*

Suddenly, when Andreas turns and runs to the exit, I have a choice to make. As a journalist, I've been writing about resistance, wondering how I might react if a chance to resist presented itself, and now, although I hesitate—and I admit that my resolve momentarily wavered. I was a mother, with two children, and the choice presented to me meant losing my children—because of the gunfire and the sirens and the sense of panic, when Andreas pushes open the glass double doors and runs outside I join him. I cram myself in the getaway car, and once the car drives off the world I used to know was left behind. At a gas station I called a friend, asked her to pick my kids up at school, not knowing when I would see them again, not knowing our escape would be successful. And because it was, I was charged with attempted murder. A reward was put on my head, for the capture of my body, and the movie *Bonnie and Clyde* had come out a few years earlier, in 1967, and like Bonnie and Clyde, I was now part of a gang, rebels like them, but I had a cause, and because I'd broken the law, because we all did, the headlines turned us into outlaws, made us mythic, and the first thing we did was give our gang a name. The Red Army Faction. We used the German word *fraktion* to indicate our solidarity with *other* people struggling against oppression, and because we had no goods to sell or services to offer, along with targeting military installations, we also robbed banks. Gudrun was ruthless, and Andreas was a petty criminal, possibly a psychopath, so the terrorist life, a life without empathy, came easy to them. I'd always thought of myself as a pacifist, always been anxious, the kind of person who didn't know what to do with her hands. Some people actually said I wasn't very good at terrorism. Which is why I dedicated myself so fervently. It's why I made sure the gang named itself after me. And it's possible that Gudrun was jealous. I was a writer so I became the de facto voice of the gang, the one who said, *If one sets a car on fire, that is a criminal offence. If one sets hundreds of cars on fire, that is political action.* Our logo was a cartoon submachine gun, with bold lettering, and when I issued statements I made it clear that we meant business, that business meant violence, that violence was how we disrupted the daily routines of people; we made those daily routines dangerous. Chaos was an inexpensive way to fight the power that abhor chaos, and *How low would you not stoop,* Brecht says, *to destroy the low?* I was willing to stoop as low as I needed, willing to hurt what I hated, willing to fight criminality by becoming a criminal. I became what I'd never been before, and I didn't want to think too hard about what it was because I didn't want to lose my resolve. When I helped plant bombs that killed human beings, that was the cost of war. And the thrill of war is the thrill of having no constraints. And with nothing to constrain us, our gang got famous, and the fame was intoxicating, but like any drug, after a while the effects wore off. The anxiety I'd felt when I was younger, now it started getting worse. I started losing weight. The constant hiding from police, the constant disguising myself, the need to separate myself from the others; it was making me, not crazy, but yes, when the story I'd created got out of my control I panicked. Every action I made, I second-guessed myself, every thought I had I doubted. I doubted the role I'd taken for myself and when finally the police, acting on a tip, came to the apartment I was using as a safe house, when they rang the doorbell, I opened the door as if I wanted to be taken away, and I was.

The two main ways to hang yourself have names. The *short drop* and the *long drop.* The long drop happens when, with a knot secured at the side of your neck, as your body falls through space, the weight of the body, when it stops falling, causes the spinal cord to snap, which causes death. First a loss of consciousness, then death, and supposedly the experience isn't painful. This was the method used to execute the people who, after the Civil War, conspired to kill, and *did* kill, Abraham Lincoln. After their guilt was determined, they were taken to a specially constructed gallows, hoods placed over their heads, nooses secured around their necks, and photographs taken at the event show the stages of the execution. Seen in order, the photos show the three men and one woman standing on the wooden platform, and then the hatch door beneath their feet opens up, and the photos that capture them mid-fall are blurry, but in the final photo their lifeless bodies hang in the so-called breeze. In the prison yard you can see the spectators, dressed for the event, the men in hats, the women in long dresses, some with parasols, and the crowd seems to turn away from what just happened, careless and unaware, like Brueghel's famous horse, turning to one another and casually talking, smiling and amused like people at a carnival or a circus. It's the same almost jovial unconcern you see on the faces of people photographed at American lynchings. And we can say that the participants there were depraved, but the whole culture was depraved. Newspapers announced the event, politicians officiated, and because it was a form of terrorism they didn't bother with gallows. And the *short drop* is just what it sounds like. The distance a person drops, with a noose around the neck, is short. Whether standing on a chair or sitting on the back of a horse, when the chair is removed and the horse runs off, the weight of the falling body tightens the noose, blocking the trachea, constricting the jugular vein and the carotid artery, and a lot of anatomical technology is involved as the person struggles to get air, to get blood to flow where it ought to be flowing, and when that doesn't happen, after an agonizing ten or twenty minutes, the person dies.

I left no suicide letter, but I did keep a notebook in prison. While my lawyers pleaded for leniency, I wrote about the feeling of being in solitary confinement. *The feeling, one's head explodes (the feeling, the top of the skull will simply split, burst open)—the feeling, one's spinal column presses into one's brain.* Some of my entries are confusing because I was confused: it's a human condition, and I was recording it, my mental and emotional disintegration. I was charged with four counts of murder, no possibility of parole, no contact with my friends, if they *were* my friends, and worst of all, the new and beautiful life I imagined I wanted, I'd failed to live it, and because I'd failed, and because I couldn't return to my old life, or any life, life was impossible to live. What choice did I have? I was talking to myself, not wanting to answer myself but my answer was clear. I had no choice but to die. So I said. To myself. And no one was there to watch me in my cell, and no camera recorded what I did. So you have to believe what I'm saying. Some people believe I hanged myself. Some suspect that someone else was involved, a guard who hated me, or was paid, and I say *hanged*, as in *the bitch was hanged*, and there's a painting of me, from a photograph, showing me from the side, dead, face up on the floor, my dark hair like a pillow, the bruise of the noose like a necklace adorning my neck. My eyes are closed, my lips parted, and when they later removed my brain and examined it, trying to learn the reason I did what I did, naturally nothing was found. Only a piece of metal, a remnant of an operation I'd had when I was younger, a girl, a metal clamp meant to cut off the blood supply to a tumor. Maybe that had affected me, distorting my common sense, short-circuiting what they now call my executive functioning. I once said, *The act of liberation is the act of annihilation.* I would have preferred a bullet to the brain but I didn't have a gun. And because I only had the window in my prison cell I had to use the short-drop technique to hang myself. Instead of a rope I used prison towels. I'd been collecting them surreptitiously until, on a day in 1976, either cloudy or sunny, I had no idea, I tied the towels together. I didn't need that many. I just had to loop the end of one around a bar of the metal grate that covered the small square window in my cell, the only source of light except for a bulb I couldn't control, and it's funny, because death is something I *could* control. My attempt to eradicate injustice had failed. My weakness hadn't transformed into anything, except more weakness, which felt like pain, a physical pain that throbs so deep in my bones that I can't even tell where it comes from, an ache that vibrates in my literal heart, and even more in my metaphorical heart, a heart that wants to burst, or implode, and yes, I still had my daughters, somewhere. I'd broken off contact. With them. And with everyone. That's how I could concentrate so completely on getting the end of the threadbare towel attached to the window grate, securing my makeshift noose with a good solid knot. I had a little trouble standing on my one chair, tying the towel around my neck, getting the knot as tight as I wanted, cinching the worn cotton cloth against my skin, but then, with the noose secure, the moment before I kicked away the chair, when I looked out of my eyes to the room in front of me, my cell like my room in the house when I was a child, like a room in my mind, I was ready to leave.

Yvonne Rainer, still from *Trio A (The Mind is a Muscle, Part I)*, 1978.

Trio A

The stage is bare except for a woman, the floor below her, the air around her, and for the duration of the dance, as she bends an arm or lifts a leg, her body seems to speak to her, or really it's speaking to itself, telling itself when to turn or jump, and because the woman is attuned to her body, inhabiting a space completely inside her body, although she's supposed to be expressionless, and she *is* expressionless, she seems to be having a good time.

The film of Yvonne Rainer performing *Trio A* was made in 1978, twelve years after she originally danced it, and roughly forty years before I started imagining what it must have felt like. And feels like. And when I say *having a good time* I mean the kind of enjoyment that comes when you're so engaged with performing a task at hand that you forget yourself, leaving behind ideas of who you used to be, or who you think you are. And *The Mind Is a Muscle.* That's what Rainer called her dance, and the problem is stretching that muscle. Actually, the problem is locating the muscle, and then, having found it, letting it relax, letting all those ideas inside the muscle thaw and dissolve, and like a tin man in a fairy tale, arms rusted, legs corroded, or tin *woman*, as the rust begins melting a quasi-electrical current passes through the tightness and stagnation, and whether it's a woman or a man the axe, poised, mid swing, ready to come down and chop the wood but not coming down because, although the action might be physically and even emotionally fulfilling, the outcome is unknown. And because it's unknown the muscles contract; they stiffen, and the axe doesn't move because your mind really *is* a muscle.

I imagine Yvonne Rainer dancing in that short silent film, filling herself with uncertainty as a way to empty her mind of everything she already knew, or wanted. And being empty, she could then be possessed by what might resonate in her, something we call *greater than her* but it's not greater; and it's not lesser; it's what she is, or was, and that's the rub. Who she was is constantly changing. Arriving in New York in 1956, she was full of ambition, ready to make her mark, and because dancing was a way to do that, she studied people she admired, dancers and artists, and even the people she didn't admire had something to teach. The technique of Martha Graham, for instance, was rooted in a movement style that valorized an emotional life that didn't align with Yvonne's emotional life. And in 1965, in reaction against the authority of that style, protesting the constraints it put on her body, she said no. No to spectacle and virtuosity, no to magic and make-believe, no to both the heroic and the antiheroic; and the point was not to be new or radical. Her manifesto was meant to clarify what was obvious to her, that dance should be free to be something it wasn't before.

Sometimes when I'm writing, when I think an idea is about to appear but the words I have don't quite reveal it, I get impatient. I get critical, judging both the idea and the words, inhibiting their inclination to expand and connect. And I understand the necessity of constraint, that wanting is one thing and not getting what you want is a fact of life, but still. I want my life to expand into moments that aren't just reiterations of what I already know. And it ought to be possible. I remember the first time I ever rented a car, standing at a counter, exchanging my driver's license for a set of car keys. I remember the expansion in my chest, a tingling along the front of my spine as I slid into the newish seat of what for me was an undiscovered experience, driving alone in a car, my hands on the wheel, the windows open, the air and the car and even the world passing outside the windshield seemed to intimate the presence of something almost divine, and because that experience didn't last forever, I'm looking for moments when it did, or does, or almost does, when the performance of self evaporates into a performance of what I don't even know I am.

Any story, if it challenges how we choose to be in the world, can give us a reason to try something new, to jolt us or jostle us, and what I'm trying to do is see in Yvonne, a story of how to be, a way that worked once, and now, although a story doesn't change any-thing, by letting a moment from the past evolve into something different, maybe it can. Yvonne was thirty years old when *Trio A* burst out of her. Or really, it *evolved* out, churning and gestating and eventually solidifying into an experience of life she was able to embody and express in her dance. And fortunately she made the film, evidence of how a body discovers what being can be. Her choreography shows both an experience, and a way to live inside that experience. And I say *inside* because the choreography is a container. And being a container, it seems as if it might be possible, by teaching our bodies to inhabit the container, even if it's only for a few short minutes, to learn the experience.

In the spring of 2017 I decided to take a class. Along with about fourteen dancers and ex-dancers, at a performance space on the Lower East Side of Manhattan, in an airless room with a vinyl floor, I enrolled in an introductory workshop called *Learning Trio A*. It was a class that would, by teaching us the individual moves of the dance, give substance to the video we'd all seen of Yvonne, dancing. I signed a contract stipulating that I wouldn't teach *Trio A* or perform *Trio A* in the future. We were told to wear shoes because Yvonne had danced the dance in shoes, and at the first meeting, along with the other dancers, I put on my sweatpants, tied my shoes, and I wondered about an audition process that might weed out uncoordinated people. But the teacher wanted a range of experiences, including my *inexperience*. So I sat on the floor, spread my legs, and pretended to stretch like the other dancers.

And I *did* stretch, reaching out, not very far but feeling the front of my spine expanding as the teacher walked between us, reminding us that the sixteen-millimeter film of Yvonne, dancing in her black shirt and pants, was only a recording, made years after the original event, shot from a single angle. Learning the dance by watching a recording of the dance would have been impossible. Imperceptible details connected every movement of the dance, and only certain people knew those details. The teacher was part of a lineage, having learned the dance from Yvonne herself, and for us, a way to become part of that lineage, to inherit, if that's possible, the physical experience of dancing like Yvonne, was to become Yvonne.

The first step, they say, if you want to change yourself, is to know yourself. And although that's not absolutely true, by learning the steps of *Trio A*, I was getting to know what my mind was doing, how it wanted things and rejected things, and because the mind is a muscle I kept practicing. In French they call it *repetition*, and the theory is, by repeating an action over and over, knowledge is absorbed by the body. In English we say *rehearse*, the hearse being a vehicle that carries the dead to the place where the body is buried, planted like a seed, and it also reminds me of hearing. Not so much *re*-hearing as hearing for the first time, which requires listening, which requires being empty enough to attend to the part of the dance that's invisible, therefore difficult to think about. Sometimes, when I was practicing the dance, my mind would wander off, following a thought that led in one direction while my body, having other thoughts, was taking me in another direction, and learning the dance means yoking the two together, getting the mind to lodge inside the body, and the body to lodge inside itself, and when I lifted my leg or flexed my foot I felt these movements affecting me. I was learning them *by heart* as they say, and *the heart has reasons* they also say, and muscle memory is just that, the muscles remembering what they'd never done before.

On the first day of the *Trio A* workshop the teacher told us, forget what you already know. I wasn't what they called *a mover*, but I did have my habits of moving, ways I'd trained my body to be, and because those habits would get in the way of learning the dance, I had to begin by letting them go. Beginnings are important; they mark a moment between what has been, and what is about to be, a moment when intention coalesces into action. When I stood with the other participants on the black, slightly padded floor, I tried to focus my intention. At the beginning of the dance you're supposed to just stand there, at a right angle to where the audience would be watching, letting yourself get acclimated to the space, to the fact of your body occupying space—and then you move. You bend your legs while simultaneously turning your head to the left, letting your arms swing loosely in their sockets, three times, back and forth across your body, then you pivot on your left foot and step with your right, and with the sole of that foot on the floor, with the left foot perched on its toe behind you, you raise your arms to shoulder level and move them in small, controlled counterclockwise circles. Practicing these moves, and perfecting them, was meant to get us to a place in which, when we bent our legs, the mind wasn't telling the body what to do, or what it *should* do. There was to be no volition. At a certain point the legs would just bend, and because there's no music in *Trio A*, when we stood on the rubbery floor and practiced the dance, although we weren't all in unison, we moved more or less together, bending and turning and opening our arms, and every so often the teacher corrected us. At the beginning of the dance, during a moment when I was supposed to turn my head while swinging my arms, apparently I also turned my torso. I was told to stabilize my ribs, keep my sternum facing forward, let the spiral happen in my neck. The teacher's assistant was a young woman with very good posture who walked up to me, held my chest between her hands, one hand on my breastplate, the other between my shoulder blades, and demonstrated to my body the details that made the dance what it was. Part of any learning is learning to trust the teacher, including an assistant teacher, and although I could feel a resistance in my body, I submitted to the adjustments she made, letting her pull me away from postural habits I didn't even know I had.

When you think about moving your arm, the arm that comes into consciousness is part of a previous gesture, part of a movement that, even if it's forgotten, informs what comes next. Like the Judson Memorial Church. In the early 1960s the old brick building on Washington Square transformed itself, becoming an incubator where people who wanted to try something new could actually *try something new*. It's where Yvonne originally presented *Trio A*, where the Judson Dance Theater got its name, and certain historical moments are like that, periods when idealism coalesces, when communities arise. And the performers who danced at the Judson probably didn't even realize it was happening. Or maybe they did. Yvonne would later say about that time, "There was new ground to be broken and we were standing on it." Yvonne Rainer and Trisha Brown and Lucinda Childs were all part of a workshop, led by a teacher named Robert Dunn. On July 6, for the end-of-the-workshop performance, because Merce Cunningham's studio wasn't big enough, and because the 92nd Street Y wasn't interested, the so-called First Concert of Dance happened at the Judson Church. Because they didn't have money for costumes or sets, the dancers took what they had, their bodies, and their bodies became the tools they used to obliterate the boundaries between art and life, between performer and choreographer, and even the audience was invited to participate in a transformation that, although it was a different time then, might still be possible.

Trisha Brown made a dance in 1971 called *Roof Piece*. Dancers were positioned on various rooftops across downtown Manhattan, and in photographs made at the time you can see them, standing on their individual rooftops, watching the other rooftops and waiting.

The dance was transmitted from roof to roof, and the dancers were waiting to see what the dance would be, what they would copy and thereby transmit to the next dancer, who would copy them, each dancer replicating the dance they saw and by dancing it, sending it to the body that was waiting. The rooftop was a prop, an obstacle that physicalized the distance between them by physicalizing the time between what they did, then, and even now, how experience gets communicated across that gap is still a question.

In one of her essays on photography, Susan Sontag quotes Diane Arbus, who talks about becoming like a soldier, crawling under what seemed like a barbed wire fence, getting behind the enemy line to do the work of the artist. "I am creeping forward on my belly," she says, "like they do in war movies." She knew the danger, the "stricken feeling where you perfectly well can get killed," and she was willing to take the risk in order to become the person who got the perfect photograph.

I thought that by taking this piece of history, *Trio A*, and reimagining it, I could reimagine myself. It could have been anything, a sport, a martial art; even the words I'm writing would do the trick. Because it's not a trick. In deciding to imagine Yvonne, not virtually but actually, to see and hear and feel how dance can be like life, the trick, once you've chosen a life, is to commit. When I write a word, because the word gets its meaning from the words around it, there's always the question of which word, or grouping of words, will lead to the meaning I want. And often, not knowing what meaning I want, I don't know how to say it. And how can I say anything about a life that wasn't mine, and isn't mine, and can't be mine because I'm limited by my own perspective. And feeling those limitations I get frustrated, stymied. I get lost, like now, feeling I don't quite deserve to decide what comes next. I remember reading the *I Ching* when I was younger, a yellow, clothbound book I kept on a shelf, and I remember the narrator of the book always talking about *perseverance* or *persevering*, how belief in an action connects it to other actions, how a word finds meaning in relation to other words, and if you persevere and follow those words, and believe that something will come next, although the process is often haphazard, something *does* come next.

Trisha Brown. Trisha Brown was a dancer. Trisha Brown was a dancer who, when she was almost thirty-five, created a piece called, appropriately, *Accumulation*. And the dance begins like that, with the dancer lifting her forearms, rotating her thumbs inward and outward until, at a certain point, she adds a second gesture, extending her arms, and then she goes back to the first gesture, rotating her thumbs, adding the second gesture, and eventually a third gesture is added, and a fourth, and the piece accretes like that, or accrues, or literally it accumulates, gesture after gesture, each one triggered by the one that came before. One then one-plus-two then one-plus-two-plus-three, and Brown referred to the form as a "perfect dance machine," the machine being the conceptual armature on which the dancer could replicate what seems like perfection but is more like choicelessness. It's about doing the gesture and trusting the gesture, and a lot of people at the time, musicians and artists and dancers, believed that by fully inhabiting a given action, meaning would accrue. Chance and indeterminacy were important ideas because any action could become transformative. And when I watch the videos of *Accumulation*, I love the feeling of being mesmerized, not by the gestures of the dance but by the pattern of the gestures, by the arms and bodies moving in ways that seem familiar, and *are* familiar, and then become unfamiliar, changing into something but I don't know *what*.

Man Walking Down the Side of a Building. That's the name of a Trisha Brown dance, made in 1970, in which a person, her husband at the time, adjusted his physical relation with the world by walking down the side of a brick building. There were ropes holding him up, and pulleys, and a camera must have been perched on a fire escape because I've seen the photographs of people looking up from a SoHo courtyard as the man slowly tips over the edge of the building's roof, changing his position form vertical to horizontal, and when he takes his first few steps down the side of the building I can feel, or imagine I feel, what it felt like to change perspective entirely. It wasn't just gravity but the habit of gravity, the attachment to what had seemed real before, being replaced by the new reality of being no longer supported by the earth, being supported by nothing, nothing but wires and ropes, and because they were jerry-rigged, the possibility of falling and dying must have been in his mind, and his body, as he walked down the bricks. Without the familiarity of gravity holding him up, he seems to be half flying, or wanting to fly, and whatever parts of the inner ear cause us to proprioceive ourselves in a certain way, when that was changed, everything else must have changed. Not everything. The title of the piece is *Man Walking Down the Side of a Building*, and the question I have is why didn't Trisha walk down the building herself? It was her idea, to turn everything on its head, including gravity. Not on its head exactly, but by changing the way we perceive the world, by literally turning it ninety degrees, the dance was asking us how, after substituting a new conception for an old one, do you then let the old conception die?

Sometimes, walking down a stretch of sidewalk, especially if I'm in an unknown city, deserted if possible, I close my eyes. I take a mental picture of the path in front of me and let my memory of the path become the path. I note where the obstacles are, a hole in the sidewalk or some forgotten dog shit, and I walk like that, blind but trusting my memory. Sometimes, instead of closing my eyes I open them, trying to imagine my mind, instead of thinking, instead of liking and disliking and judging, just noticing, just choicelessly seeing the world, and mainly it's hearing, letting the consciousness that resides in the front of my brain move to the back, to the so-called reptilian part of my brain. Because the sense of sight is usually dominant, consciousness tends to be forward facing. To live in the back of the brain means living in an altered world of pure perception, and sometimes when I do it I can hear birds chirping in trees, or cars going by, and when people approach me, walking toward me on the sidewalk, although I would like to retain my newly altered consciousness, instead of concentrating on the world, I turn my attention back to myself, to how I appear. Not wanting to seem like a crazy person, I find myself inhibiting myself, reverting to habits I know, my body contracting and losing the pleasure of expansion and connectedness, and instead of responding to events in a clear and honest way, I act in a way that I *think* is normal, performing a version of who I assume I'm supposed to be.

In her instructions for dancing *Trio A*, Yvonne stipulated that the dancers never acknowledge the audience. In the video of her performing the dance, at no point does she raise her eyes to regard the camera that's watching and recording her. This was partly an attempt to free herself from the judgments of the spectator, to negate the power of anyone who supposedly knew more, or knew better; and it's also a way to negate your*self*. You say no to the part of yourself that submits to craving, which is for attention, forgoing what Yvonne called "seduction of [the] spectator by the wiles of the performer." Because she distrusted the spectator's desire, she also distrusted her *own* desire to woo them, to win them over, and like Brecht, who distrusted the audience's easy identification with the actor, Yvonne sought to take her personality out of the equation.

How marvelous it all does seem, in retrospect. That's Susan Sontag talking about the 1960s, about its boldness, its optimism. And it's easy, looking back, to forget that the people who were part of that optimism were just living their lives. They weren't necessarily better lives, or happier, but as the Wizard of Oz might've said, they had *one thing we haven't got.* A sense that what they were doing mattered. That's why Yvonne, when she danced *Trio A*, because she didn't want to be distracted by what *didn't* matter, closed her eyes. What mattered was paying attention, maintaining her balance by attuning her mind-slash-muscle to what was happening, moment by moment, not knowing what that would be but noticing her responses and connecting her shifting intention from what had happened a second ago to what was happening now. That's one reason I enrolled in the *Trio A* workshop. To shift in myself what had come to feel stuck, worn out. My desires had become, not like ghosts, but they didn't seem to have a place. They were old, therefore probably corrupt, and whether it's me or forces acting on me, it was time to be shown, by someone who knew, that I could experience desire undistracted by the influence of other desires. That's why I listened to the teacher describe a complicated dance that happened fifty years earlier. It's why I would sit on the floor at the end of each two-hour session, my legs forming a V, stretching the muscles around my pelvis while the memory of the dance still percolated in my body. I tried to release the entire length of my spine, letting my body connect to my brain and adjust to a new way of being. And because there were people around me, talking, getting dressed, possibly watching me, as I sat on the bones of my pelvis, reaching my fingertips out in front of me, although I wanted to be watched I also wanted to be *free* of that watching, and so I closed my eyes. I closed my eyes the way babies, because their sense of self is so tenuous, when they close their eyes, believe they disappear.

In 1960 John Cage, the composer, appeared on a television quiz show called *I've Got a Secret*. Its format was to introduce people with unusual skills or occupations and to have a panel of celebrities guess who they were. On one particular night it was Cage, tall, relaxed, wearing a simple suit and a dark tie, and the host pretended to be worried that experimental music wouldn't make sense to the studio audience; he apologized for the laughter that might follow. But Cage didn't mind laughter. He preferred it, he said, to tears.

And I don't remember if anyone laughed, but for him the format was changed. Instead of fielding questions from the celebrity panel, he would *perform* his secret. *Water Walk* was the title, and that's what it was, him walking around an assortment of props, making sounds with the various everyday objects. Originally, it involved radios, playing the static between the stations, but disputes with the union, whose job was to turn *on* the radios, meant he had to play without them. He had a bathtub and a kettle, a potted plant and a watering can, and he started by pouring water into the tub. There were seltzer bottles and steam whistles, and although it all related tangentially to water, it wasn't the kind of music an audience would necessarily understand. Or even like. But he wasn't asking them to like it. Just pay attention. That's how Zen monks do it, just hear whatever exists, without judging it or naming it, just listening, and after the piece was over the host had a question. Was it music? And Cage didn't have an answer. A good lawyer would probably have had an answer but Cage, like a good Zen monk, was asking a different question.

People at the time were staging events they called Happenings. In them, the question of what something meant was answered by making it up, by inventing or reinventing or setting up a context and then, by queering the context, making meaning interesting again. When the audience stepped into a Happening they weren't necessarily naked, but in the same way a performer is naked on stage, they became actors in pieces of theater that had a beginning, an end, and between them nobody knew what would happen. In 1960 Simone Forti staged a dance called *See Saw* in which the two performers performed their movements perched on a literal see-saw, a plank of wood that was balanced on a sawhorse fulcrum. The prop was a narrative device, an invented obstacle that would focus their minds on the task at hand, thereby freeing their bodies to make the dance into metaphor. In photographs of the performance you can see a young Yvonne Rainer and a slightly older Robert

Morris using the plank and its precarious balance to tell, not a story, but whatever their relationship might have been in so-called real life, it was on display during the dance. The ends of the seesaw were attached to the walls with large, rubber band-like straps that kept the seesaw more or less horizontal; but not completely. In one photo, Morris is shown squatting on the plank, his feet solidly on the floor, and because he had the advantage of weight, Rainer had to adjust, and she does, scooting out to the edge of the wood, tuning in to his changes of mood and intention, and that was the task, to negotiate a balance that was partly a balance of power.

When we practiced *Trio A* during the workshop, dancing on the rubber floor in the basement studio, because everyone followed their own internal timing, some of the dancers were faster than others. And being one of the slower ones, I was always trying to catch up. My mind, instead of trusting my muscles, was thinking about the phrase I was supposed to be doing. And that's why Yvonne didn't want us thinking about phrases. The dance, she said, was continuous—"no one thing is any more important than any other,"—but because I was trying to figure out what step was supposed to follow from the step I'd just finished, I wasn't feeling it. By *it* I mean the mental state connected to the dance that would connect me to a larger . . . and I would almost say larger *picture* but part of the point of the dance was that it *wasn't* a picture, wasn't something to be viewed and judged, but instead experienced, by the performer who'd internalized the movement. Not that Yvonne performed in empty theaters. People came to watch her, and she let them watch, and when it was announced, about halfway through the workshop, that we would perform the dance for each other, I was willing to try. Willing but underprepared, and my teacher helped me prepare by giving me a little more attention, by calling out to me what move came next, not like a mother but it felt like a mother's concern, and I wanted her to be proud. The movements in *Trio A* are called pedestrian, but it wasn't as if anyone walking down the street could perform them. Some were very *un*-pedestrian, some very difficult, at least for me, and although I needed my teacher's help I didn't want her seeing me when I was lost, or doing the wrong movement. I wanted her to see me when, now and then, I found myself doing the right movement, found myself *in the groove* as they used to say, inhabiting the dance and letting the parts I'd managed to memorize change the part of myself that had put them in memory. Turning my head, for instance, or looking over my left shoulder, letting the memory of what I was doing move from my head to my body, lodging itself in my muscles and tendons and sometimes I imagined I felt the spirit of Yvonne as it entered me, an experience that would have been transcendental except the minute those moments appeared I noticed them—not just noticed, I enjoyed them and admired them, and admired myself for having them—and if anyone was watching, I wanted to show them what I'd done, wanted to show my so-called stuff, and the teacher told me that I had a nice verticality, and that Yvonne had that too, and it's funny when you get a compliment, and calling me vertical seemed like a compliment, you begin to play to that compliment.

There were bound to be moments when, in the course of learning the dance, having practiced a certain section over and over, I felt I was getting it. But mostly I didn't. Mostly, in the middle of forgetting where I was I would look over, knowing we weren't supposed to look, and sometimes, seeing my teacher sitting on the plastic chair, the mirrored wall behind her, I would imagine Yvonne. In my mind, an older version of Yvonne was standing beside the chair, watching me, either approving or disapproving. And because Yvonne was the progenitor of the dance, by performing *her* dance, *for* her, how could I not be performing a *version* of her? My daughter does the same thing with me. She imitates me, repeating what I say, or if I do something, she does it after me, showing me what she's done, and of course she imitates me. She imitates everyone.

And with Yvonne, I was the child, imitating her and making mistakes but like a good enough mother, she let me make them. That's how you learn, and because I tend to be careful, meaning it's difficult for me to forget my mistakes and move on, every mistake I made when I danced *Trio A* made it harder for me to remember where I was in the dance, to remember the steps and take the steps, and even with an imaginary Yvonne watching over me, because I felt her watching over me, my body refused to do what my mind was asking it to do. It rebelled, saying *no* to my mind's authority, and *no* to Yvonne's authority, fending off the power I'd given her to show me the way, which wasn't *my* way, certainly not the *only* way, not even a very enjoyable way. But I stubbornly slugged it out, doggedly repeating gestures I only half believed would cement in me the habit I wanted, one that Yvonne had demonstrated, years ago, and maybe I was getting tired. Even Yvonne got tired. In her autobiography she talks about her relationship with Robert Morris, an older artist she lived with and probably loved, a successful sculptor and performer who she knew was having affairs, cheating on her with other women, and she didn't want to be cheated on, but she was dependent on him, both of them dependent on each other for the life they were living, and one of the unspoken rules of that life was: the one with less dependency wins. And maybe Yvonne had lovers, too, but his betrayal, what it felt like, must have devastated her. There was a suicide attempt, an extended foray into psychotherapy, none of which helped her solve the bigger problem of who she was and how she fit in the world. And when I say *what choice did she have* it isn't a rhetorical question. One day, under the spell of her desperation, she walked into an alley, probably infested, reeking of urine, and she took off her clothes. It was inappropriate, she knew that, and she did it *because* it was inappropriate, because she wanted to be noticed, not praised necessarily but her desperation needed an outlet, and the policeman who found her took her to Bellevue Hospital, a hospital for insane people, for people with problems she didn't want, and when Robert Morris came back they probably tried to change, probably promised each other they *would* change, and maybe she never intended to kill herself but how does a person change?

At some point the *Trio A* workshop was going to be over. At some point, having absorbed the lessons in Yvonne's choreography, I would break away from her influence. But that point hadn't yet come. I was still learning the moves, still struggling with the steps, still trying to imagine Yvonne, standing with her perfect verticality, telling me how to dance a dance that isn't even mine. It's hers. *My* dance is another dance, a dance only *I* can dance like only *she* could dance *Trio A*, a dance from the past, from a moment in time that doesn't exist anymore, which makes dancing it now almost impossible. And maybe impossibility is what I need. Sontag says *the most interesting characteristic of the time now labeled the Sixties was that there was so little nostalgia*, and maybe what I need is an end to the constant looking back and struggling with what's already done, worn out, a vaguely remembered reiteration of something I've lost, which seems to be what I always struggle with, constantly and unsuccessfully, and although the failure doesn't destroy me, it is a kind of destruction, a kind of small bomb going off and after the explosion, if it doesn't kill you, after you recover, maybe the destruction is necessary.

On the last day of the workshop we were going to perform our individual versions of the dance. Over the course of two weeks we'd taken in this information, using it to inform our bodies, and now we sat on the floor, our backs to the mirrored wall, and the teacher, who looked Irish or Celtic, sat in her folding chair. The first volunteers were the dancers who'd studied Yvonne, the ones who knew the steps, and although I wanted to postpone my own performance, I didn't want to postpone too long. I didn't want to be the final performer, my ineptitude sticking in people's minds. So about halfway through the examination I volunteered. It wasn't an examination, but I stood up, walked to the place on the floor where the dance was supposed to begin. Years before I'd taken a workshop with Lucinda Childs, a Judson dancer who'd worked with Yvonne, and I had a pretty good idea what it meant to begin, to stand on the spot where we all had to start, stage left, and I took my time getting ready, acclimating myself to the fact that people were watching. Yvonne expected the dance to be seen, but without the dancer corrupted by that seeing. That's why I closed my eyes. I let my body relax as much as it could, noticing the heels of my feet, the mounds of my toes inside my shoes, and the person who'd gone before me had done a pretty good job of imitating Yvonne, but she hadn't quite abandoned herself. She'd done all the steps, the steps I was about to do, or try to do, and I was trying not to compare myself with her. The teacher was half kneeling in her chair, one leg curled under her, and that's when I felt the moment begin. I bent my knees about thirty degrees, turned my head, and because this was the part I'd practiced, this was my chance to give my body the reins, as they say, and like watching a leaf blown by the breeze, I felt my arms swinging in their sockets, the momentum of the swing propelling me forward, my left leg rising and stepping, and all I had to do was keep going, stay out of my way and follow the momentum, letting my mind have its thoughts but not be distracted by those thoughts, taking the next step, and the next, and when I stretched my arms out like an airplane, moving them in circles, I could imagine the air circling around my hands, the trajectory of the circle leading to a turn that led to a difficult move for me, standing on one foot, bending the back of my neck while lifting one leg up, then down, then rounding my back, my whole spine curling in, and although it wasn't perfect, what was supposed to happen was basically happening. I'd forgotten about the teacher, and about the other dancers, my peripheral vision seeing everything but unfocused, but with total focus, not thinking about what came next because what came next would come, would call itself into being, acting *on* me and *in* me, and at some point I came out of the trance to notice how good it felt. And when I noticed myself noticing, that's when I tried to get back to the dance, back to the muscles and bones in my body. And that *trying* is what I had trouble with, the *trying* that becomes an impediment, that posits a thing you're trying to achieve or grasp, separate from what you are, and trying to let go of that trying is of course just another form of trying. But what can you do except try. So I tried to listen. Listen, I thought, to my feet on the floor, and the sound of the air in the studio, the cars outside on Grand Street, or East Broadway, it doesn't matter which because it isn't about *what* you hear, it's the state of hearing, of perception becoming just that, perception, and when I turned, landed again on one foot, although I remembered to flex the foot I forgot if I was supposed to look to my left *before* taking a step, or after the step, and what was the next step? And not knowing what I was doing, but knowing a jump was supposed to happen, at some point, I did a little leap, which was more a stumble, but a moderately graceful stumble, and I was still listening, still hearing the trucks honking outside the windows. And I'm thinking about Hedy Lamarr because, besides being known as the most beautiful woman in the world, she invented, along with a composer of modernist music, what was known as a frequency-hopping missile-guidance system. In World War II, the radio signals that guided American torpedoes were being intercepted, sending them off course, and Hedy Lamarr must have known that a different system was needed because she figured out a code, like player-piano music, that directed the torpedoes with a frequency the enemy couldn't figure out, seemingly random, and if I am going to inhabit my life instead of just performing it, I need to change the frequency of the signals I'm sending myself. Although I could hear the trucks on the street, honking, and the sirens doing what sirens do, my feet on the floor weren't getting the signal. They were losing the thread, or I was, of the dance, and because the thread was invisible, the more I looked for it the more invisible it seemed to be, so invisible that I forgot the thread, forgot the admonitions of the teacher who was watching this half-deflated puppet, which was me, half-heartedly trying to *be* some thing or *do* some thing, and because the thing wasn't me, was outside of me, I stopped. I raised my eyes to the mirror in front of me, and although I believed the old adage about the tough getting going when the going gets tough, I didn't go anywhere. I stood there, dumb in both senses of the word, and when the teacher clapped, signaling the end of my dance, although everyone joined her, nothing had changed. The clapping didn't mean anything because I didn't deserve it.

My attempt to learn *Trio A* was bound to fail, partly because, having imagined a euphoria that Yvonne must have felt, all I saw was possibility. And possibilities are fine but I demanded them. And because I did, the desire to incarnate myself as a version of Yvonne was impossible. Because I wasn't Yvonne. And can't be Yvonne. And I can't be myself because every time I try to be what I am, whatever that is, something demands I be something else. That's not right. It's *me* doing the demanding. And failing to satisfy my demands only makes me more adamant. Writing this essay, I know, isn't going to change the person who's writing it, but still I keep trying. And it's not about failing better, it's just failing differently. In the dance, even if I managed to move my hand in the way I'd been taught, I never felt the satisfaction that moving my hand that way was supposed to engender. My mind was directing the moving, and because the memory of that moving, instead of residing in my body and liberating my mind, stayed in my mind, I kept repeating the same habits, turning them into stories that acted on me and molded me, and because it was my story I couldn't get out. Although I would sometimes relax enough to enjoy my ignorance and understand, briefly, the dance Yvonne had danced a lifetime ago, it didn't happen often. Most of the time I was too busy thinking about Yvonne to *be* Yvonne, and Yvonne couldn't save me, and even if she did, or maybe she did, or maybe I have the wrong body.

J. Haskell, *The author and his aunt.* 2005

A Good Jester

A few years ago,
on a book tour in Germany, after visiting the towns of Bamberg
and Hamburg, I found myself in Nürnberg. And since I had some
spare time I wandered around the historic parts of town, a bridge
and a church and the house where Albrecht Dürer, the painter, was
born. Apparently, during the war, the old town was almost totally
destroyed by Allied bombing, but then, when the war was over,
after the dust and rubble had been cleared away, the old historical structures were painstakingly re-assembled, timber by timber,
the boyhood home of Albrecht Dürer faithfully re-created, turned
into a replica of what it once had been, years ago, and now, because
the replica is good, it seems to be what it pretends to be.

The Good Person of Szechuan
is a play by the German playwright Bertolt Brecht, set in the imaginary town of Szechwan, or Szechuan, and it begins with three
mysterious gods visiting the town, searching for the eponymous
good person. The play was completed in 1941, at a time when the
good people of Brecht's native Germany seemed to have lost their
sense of direction. It's about being good in a less than perfect world,
and because Brecht didn't necessarily assume that was possible, the
gods in the play, dressed as beggars, look like carriers of disease.
They're old and ugly, and no one wants to help until they meet a
working girl named Shen Te. When they ask for a place to stay she
offers them her shabby room. And immediately it's clear to them.
They've found what they've been searching for, a mensch, a person
whose struggle includes the practice of compassion. Her life is un-
pleasant but she makes it pleasant for *them*, feeding them what she

can, thin soup, offering them blankets, and she doesn't have a bed but she tries to make them welcome. And the next day they reward her. Suddenly her pockets are full of the money she needs to buy a small tobacco shop, which means, in her mind, a chance to live the life she's dreamed about, an honest life with self-respect, and she decorates her shop with lanterns and fabric and it's thrilling to do the work of making her dream come true.

The Court Jester
is a movie from 1955 starring Danny Kaye. It's set in a quasi-medieval past where clowns and jugglers and acrobats provided the entertainment. Danny played the part of a clown, an errand boy for a traveling medicine show, and although he was trained as a dancer, and was probably a competent juggler, the primary purpose of this particular medicine show was to sell an elixir, a product that cost no money to make and whose only value was imaginary. It was called a *magic* elixir because its curative powers were mysterious. Most of the ills it supposedly cured were sexual, and once his boss had pitched the product to an audience, Danny's job was to sit behind a folding table stacked with small brown bottles, and when a woman steps up to the table and begins examining the hand-printed label, reading the ingredients, this is the moment when Danny is presented with a chance to be good. Essentially, he *is* good, and when the woman asks if the potion really works, if it actually cures headaches and hair loss and constipation, the truthful answer, aside from any placebo effect, is no. But Danny is supposed to say yes, his job to allay the customer's fear, to coax or cajole or give the woman certainty, playing the part of a salesman, selling the drug as a wonder drug, but the woman didn't want a salesman. She wanted an honest answer. And so, even as the lie rises up to the back of his throat, passing across his vocal cords and over his tongue, although he's saying the word *yes* to the woman, he very deliberately moves his head back and forth, *shaking* his head as a way to negate the yes, or qualify the yes. And it's funny when confusion happens to

someone else. The woman asks him again, *is this stuff any good*, and although a part of him—his mouth—lies to her, another part—his body—attempts to communicate something true, to himself and the woman, and because ambivalence doesn't sell elixir, when his boss sees what he's doing, Danny is fired.

The good person of Szechuan,
because she's good, when she's given the chance to *perform* her goodness, she does. And in the beginning, all goes well. But the beginning only lasts until her neighbors show up, appraising her new tobacco shop and admiring her good fortune. Naturally they want a piece of that fortune. Even people who'd spurned her in the past, by virtue of nothing, feel entitled to eat her food and smoke her golden tobacco, and because she really is a good person, she's happy to help. Not *happy*, but willing to share with the world whatever she has, which she does as much as she can but of course it's never enough. Her kindness is quickly forgotten, and because of her generosity, instead of making money, she finds herself losing more and more, and because her shop needs money to survive, she's about to lose her shop. The play was written during the war, and the atrocities it describes are the everyday atrocities that still exist, greed and the reasons for greed, and because they're endless, the good person needs help. And because no one offers her help she invents someone. She conjures up an alter ego, another self, stronger than she is, less sympathetic, less compassionate, and one day, when she's called away on a business trip, the person who relays the news to the neighbors, the person who takes over running the shop while she's gone, is her cousin. Unlike the good person, this person is disciplined, plus he's a man, ruthless enough and determined enough, and under his management the tobacco shop changes. The people who'd taken advantage of Shen don't take advantage of *him*. The shop begins making money, goes into the black, as they say, and when Shen returns from her business trip the cousin has mysteriously vanished. That's when the neighbors return, demanding

loans and smoking her tobacco and when the loans go unpaid the shop gets into financial trouble again. And that's when the cousin reappears, intervening to save the shop and save Shen, and it would probably lead to a happy ending but watching the play, seeing it performed on a stage, you realize that Shen and her cousin are never onstage at the same time. Because Shen *is* her cousin. One actor plays the part of a person playing two completely different people.

Tummler is Yiddish,
a word that translates, roughly, as raconteur, a recounter of tales. Danny Kaye was a kid from Brooklyn, a hoofer and tummler who worked his way from the Catskills to vaudeville to the movies. In the early days of television he hosted a variety show, the *Danny Kaye Show*, in which he told stories, sang songs, and acted in skits. It was a lot like vaudeville, often taped in front of a live audience, and in 1963 one of the musical numbers was a duo, a song and dance in which the guest star, Gene Kelly, famous for *Singin' in the Rain*, saunters onto the stage and the two friends, one lankier than the other, begin joking around, standing in front of a painted backdrop showing the skyline of New York City, reminiscing about show business, playfully bantering with each other as they begin, gradually, bending their knees and swinging their arms. You can see them in the video, wearing black suits with thin ties, moving across the stage, enjoying the enjoyment of inhabiting their bodies, the ease and grace, and Danny wants to know how a person dances. *Like that*, Kelly says. *You're doing it now*. Danny says, *This? This isn't dancing*. And he moves in a way to demonstrate how ordinary an everyday gesture can be, how prosaic it is. And it doesn't seem like dancing, at first. But then, after a few repetitions the gestures begin to accumulate, and transform, and Kelly tells his friend, *That's it, pal. You're doing it*. And gradually they both begin moving, not in unison, but their arms and legs are allowing the music, which is jazzy, to enter their bodies, animating them and distracting them from the cameras and lights, and although there may have been a

studio audience watching the pleasure of their performance, because the pleasure is real, they don't seem to be performing.

Apparently
a book I'd written called *American Purgatorio* became popular in
Germany, popular enough that I was invited to give readings in
various cities, usually at a consulate, and in Nürnberg, when I arrived at the American consulate I could tell a mistake had been
made. The person they'd meant to invite was someone else, someone older and more famous than I was, but with a similar-sound-
ing name. His name was Jonathan, which is what they called me,
which was slightly confusing, and confusion is funny when it happens to someone else but now, seeing my confusion, they seemed
to overcompensate. They offered me candies from a bowl, a glass
of white wine, and it's not that they *lavished* me with attention, but
the attention they gave me was pleasant. It felt good when Marian,
one of the consulate workers, told me she'd fallen in love with my
book. She was planning to read it again, she said, and although
it wasn't *my* book, I sat with her at her blond desk and we talked about writing, and about Nürnberg, and *Die Meistersinger von
Nürnberg* is an opera about deception and self-deception, about a
person, motivated by love, who wants to become a master singer.
But how do you do that? How do you sing your emotional life if
that life isn't yours? Later, when Marian gave me a tour of the city,
I never got around to telling her that the book she liked so much
wasn't mine. We went to the parade grounds on the outskirts of
town where the Third Reich held its rallies, and she took me to
the town's historic center, to Albrecht Dürer's house, obliterated by
bombs during the war, and after the war, after the destruction was
cleared away, the old historical edifice was painstakingly brought
back to life, timber by timber, turned into a replica of what it once
had been, years ago, and Marian, when she told me this story,
thought she was telling the author she thought I was. When she
sat with me at a local bierstube and talked about the parts of my

book that made her cry, although I knew I hadn't written those parts, I let her keep talking. Even when she pulled a book from her canvas tote and asked me to sign it, because I didn't want to spoil the pleasure I was having hanging out with her, I didn't say, *Oh, I'm so sorry, I think a mistake has been made.* Instead, I scribbled an illegible signature, sitting with her and drinking my beer, letting the mistake continue, hoping she would believe, just a little bit longer, that I was the person she wanted, the one she respected, and of course I knew that at some point I would have to step out of the lie I'd accidentally wandered into and return to the person I was, to the story that was actually mine. And it's not that I didn't know how. *Tell the truth.* That's what they say. And they also say, *to be of two minds is a joke when it happens to someone else.*

Danny Kaye

was usually cast as the innocent, well-meaning bystander to the story until something comes along to change the story. In *The Court Jester,* after he's fired for telling the truth, he wanders into a forest on the outskirts of town and meets a group of dissidents fighting against injustice, against a usurper king who's deposed the rightful heir to the throne, and Danny is attracted to their idealism; their optimism mirrors his own. And because he's a song-and-dance man, at the rebel camp he does a song-and-dance about an innocent, red-haired nebbish becoming a lionhearted champion of truth. He sings about mistaken identity, about people becoming, not what they seem to be, but what they aspire to be, and because he aspires to be good, he volunteers to sneak inside the castle walls and find a secret key. The key is a MacGuffin, what Alfred Hitchcock called a plot device that doesn't matter, but Danny, determined to find it, stumbles into a room where a sorceress, shaking out some pillows, accidentally hypnotizes him, casting a spell that changes him from a loose-limbed dreamer into a dashing Casanova, a Romeo or Valentino, and under the spell he gallantly swings from chandeliers until, when someone sneezes, the spell is broken.

At which point he becomes himself again, shy and unassuming, and it's funny to watch him vacillate like that, between bumbling and swashbuckling, trying to reconcile himself to an ambiguity he doesn't quite understand, hoping he might eventually find his way to a clarity, or a resolution, and when that doesn't happen, in a moment of ill-considered optimism, he agrees to participate in a joust. In *Die Meistersinger* there's also a contest, a singing contest in which an innocent beginner, inhabiting the spirit of an experienced shoemaker, defeats the seasoned professional and joins the ranks of Meistersingers. In *The Court Jester*, under the influence of the magic spell, Danny is optimistic about his chances in the joust until, when someone sneezes, he sees that he's gone off track, that his desire to be good has convinced him that he *is* good, that he's strong and chivalrous and not just a clown who, instead of a single, stable personality, has two, and he can't keep them straight because neither are stable. And confusion is funny when it happens to other people, but now Danny finds himself literally *of two minds*, each mind with a disparate nature, and juggling disparateness is called, in German, *unmöglichkeit*, which means *impossibility*, or sometimes *conundrum*, and one way to face the conundrum's confusion is to embrace the confusion. That's why the sorceress, before the joust begins, empties a vial of poison into one of chalices of mead that Danny and his opponent are supposed to drink. The plan will work if he can remember which chalice has the malice, and which brew is true. She's given him a code, a mnemonic device to help him determine which cup is the good cup, but when he steps up to the royal dais, when he looks at the two silver goblets on the table in front of him, his memory fails. And he makes a joke because that's his job, but it's hard to make light of the fact that everything you wanted to do and be will fail unless you can do something right. Which is when, because it's a comedy, the Technicolor sky opens up and a bolt of lightning strikes the armor Danny is wearing, lighting it up and magnetizing him, attracting him to anything metal. And because his opponent is wearing a breastplate made of steel, Danny is magnetically drawn to the man's iron torso. The palace guards try to separate them but because of proximity Danny is pulled, again and again, to the larger man, adhering to him and wrestling against an invisible magnetic force that feels like you're wrestling with yourself.

For the good person of Szechuan
it's already too late. At some point her goodness has become a liability, and the only way a person who wants to be good can *be* good, is to disappear. Brecht left Germany during the war and Shen, in the play, leaves her world by disappearing into a role. She becomes her cousin, and for a while the performance is successful. Just as Brecht was able to continue writing his plays in America, the good person is able to turn her shop into a thriving commercial enterprise. But any role can wear you down. Brecht, frustrated with the constant California sunshine, left his émigré enclave and went back to Berlin. The good person, although she depends on her cousin to keep the shop running, because she can never completely *become* her cousin, gets worn down. She tries to make do because that's the advice we're usually given: *put on a good face, keep a stiff upper lip, rise above the corrupted swamp that's bubbling up around you and let it not matter.* But it does matter. And when the gods reappear at the end of the play, although they can see that their good person has failed, she only failed because the choices she had were so few, so binary. The townspeople needed a certainty that can't exist and so, when they find a bundle of her clothes hidden in a cupboard, the clothes she abandoned when she became her cousin, they accuse the cousin of her murder, not knowing it's *her* they're accusing of murder, and whoever it is they put on trial, the verdict they reach at the end of the trial is guilty, of failing to be a good person.

On the outskirts of Nürnberg
are the ruins that had once been monuments to Germany's so-called thousand-year Reich, stadiums and parade grounds, and

theoretically those buildings, designed by war criminals, born of despicable and mistaken ideas, would have been torn down, demolished long ago. But they weren't. The vast Zeppelin Field, documented by Leni Reifenstahl in *Triumph of the Will*, where thousands of people swarmed together, waving their arms and their flags in celebration of those distorted ideas, has been allowed to stand, to be what it is, a failure, because that's how people learn, by failing.

Still from *The Danny Kaye Show*, October 22, 1963.

When a Woman

When a Woman Ascends the Stairs
is a Japanese movie from 1960, and in it you work at a bar
in the Ginza. You're a hostess. That means you get the men
who visit the bar to drink. That's your job, selling drinks.
It pays for your house and your clothes and the only thing is,
it's not how you want to be living your life. But you're doing it,
for now. You have your clients, your regular customers, but also
a boss who demands that you sell *more* drinks, make yourself
more attractive, and when the bartender suggests that you
open your *own* club, the idea of becoming other than what
you already are begins to germinate, expanding like a seed
inside your ribs. The only problem is, opening a nightclub
takes money. And the only way you know to *get* that money
is to ask your customers for . . . You call it a loan but it feels
more like begging, like squatting on the sidewalk with a cup
in your hand. And one of your clients is more like a friend,
a banker your own age who's fond of you, you think. And
you're fond of him. You wonder what would happen if you . . .
if *he* would ever, not fall in love with you necessarily, but
if he'd ask you to be with him you would probably say yes.
Another man from the club, a red-faced salesman from Osaka
would be happy to give you a loan but he wants collateral,
in the form of affection. It's the only currency you have but
you decline his offer. But there aren't any other offers. And
without money, your dream of becoming what you want to be
will die, will wither and die, and now it's a late spring afternoon.
You're on your way to work, standing on a train station platform,

wearing your kimono, an outfit you don't see much anymore,
and across the platform a bride, still in her wedding gown,
is posing for photos, seemingly happy, and one of the options
you have is to be like her, to let someone take care of you.
A million yen is a lot of money, but it isn't just the money.
It's desire itself that can be a disease, and instead of letting it
gnaw at you, you imagine a beautiful tree with a delicate bud
at the end of a branch, the folded petals about to expand and
transform, and that evening, as you climb the stairs to your job
at the club, you tell yourself you're willing to be patient, willing
to wait for the petals to become what they're meant to become,
but the truth is, you're tired of waiting.

A few days later you're sitting at a noodle shop,
waiting for your broth to cool, blowing into the steam,
your hope for a loan slowly slipping away, and with it,
any hope that your life might actually change. That's when
a man from the club, an awkward, balding, overweight man
walks up to your table, bows very politely and asks if he can sit.
And before you can answer yes or no he confesses that he's been
following you, watching you, which is weird but at least he's honest.
You appreciate his honesty. You let him sit. And because he's
willing to listen, you start talking, telling him about your dream
of opening a bar, of changing your life by controlling your life,
but even as you say it, the words seem almost inconceivable, as if
the clouds above your head, tired of holding in the rain, tired
of the heaviness of their memory, would say *enough*, open up,
and the blue sky that's always been there would be revealed.
And that's the problem with control. It's out of your control.
You hear stories of people who pull themselves up by their
bootstraps, but imagining that is like trying to solve a riddle
or a koan. And it *is* a koan, like finding the money you need.
So you keep talking, telling this clumsy, perspiring man about
a certain perfume, a perfume you like but can't quite afford, and

talking to him distracts you from an ache that seems to have
physicalized itself right behind your sternum, like a fist, as if
the veins that flowed to your heart got twisted, tied into knots,
and that's when this man, referring to your financial situation,
announces his intention of making a large investment.

His promise of money, you think, is an indication of
his affection. In the weeks that follow, although he's shy,
he's persistent. One night, at the end of a shift, he offers to
drive you home from the club and you acquiesce. You notice
the sound of the rain on the hood of the car, and because of
the rain, or because you're tired, it doesn't occur to you that
you're reaching out for anything. He parks his car at the side of
your house and you sit in silence. You take his awkwardness for
sincerity. His headlights are shining on the climbing vines outside
the windshield, vines you're not seeing because you're thinking
of the solitary person you've become. What would it mean to be
conjoined with another person? Couples you see on the street
seem fulfilled, more or less, but somehow your heart isn't in it.
And that's the problem. Your heart seems not to be in anything.
But you're good at listening, and by listening you become receptive,
to *what* you don't know until the man hands you a package,
a carefully wrapped box containing a bottle of perfume, the kind
you wanted but couldn't afford. And the fact that he thought of you.
That's when the twisted-up fibers behind your sternum begin to
unravel. Someone has tried to know you, to figure out what might
make you happy, and you don't want to cry but your body can't help it.
You can feel the knot in your chest, not dissolving, but yes, in a way,
and the tears in your eyes are tears not of joy but relief. The pressure
of having to choose how to be in the world is over. When you
let your head rest on his shoulder, he places his arm on
your shoulder. And vulnerability is like that, like finally
relaxing, like closing your eyes and letting yourself fall asleep.
It's hard being strong all the time. The money he promised,

he'll make sure you get it. And when he proposes marriage,
it seems like a logical step, like a way to let happiness happen,
and sadness too, all of it, simultaneously, spreading out from
the place you call your heart to the thing you call your
body. And even if your dream of independence hasn't
quite worked out, at least not yet, because you're going
to be his wife, you let him try to make love.

In the movie, you're airing out your mattress in the yard
behind your house. The morning sky is crisp, cloudless. Your
banker friend is still in your thoughts but he has obligations,
can't marry you, and anyway, now you're with someone else,
someone sweet, and being with him is not giving up, not settling
for anything. Your body will learn how a life can change, how it
can fill the empty spaces that want to be filled. That's how
it works. Love doesn't always give us a choice. Or if it does,
we don't notice. Or we hide from it. Or we fight it. In the past
you've tried to distract yourself from sadness and longing. And
when I say the air is crisp, I mean like glass, like a surface where
sadness has been wiped away. The simple task of hanging a
mattress on a fence is somehow satisfying. Before the war
you were married, and why should life stop? It doesn't. And
how it goes on is unknown but doesn't a person have to go on?
The perfume you placed behind your ear last night has blended
with the breeze from the sea. Today you plan to wash your windows,
to throw them open and welcome in a new beginning. And then
you get a call. From a woman. You hold the phone to your ear but
you're not quite sure if you're catching the name. She says a name.
It sounds like the bald man's name. She wants to meet. Is it
the bald man's sister? It's not clear. But it's not the sister.
It's his wife. You meet at the edge of the city, near a factory,
in a clearing where the rubble has been bulldozed away,
a parking lot without cars. The woman stands in the cool sun
with two young boys who play on a tricycle in the wet dirt.

She tells you she found his address book, called the numbers
and did you fall for it? You're not even listening. He does this
all the time, she says. Buys a gift, borrows a car, proposes marriage.
He's not a bad man. He wants to believe his lies but look at us.
You're not looking at anything. Inside your chest the exhalations
start to take over, small repetitive implosions, one after another,
deflating you, pulling you down and into the place in your chest
where, because you can't bear to feel it, you watch the two
little boys riding the tricycle in circles.

You can understand how a person might
look for something to blame. In your case, in the movie,
you start drinking. In the past, drinking has gotten you
out of yourself, away from whatever misery you might have
been feeling. And now seems like a perfect time for one of those
sugary, delicious cocktails. It might make the gnawing
in your chest slightly bearable. At least not completely
*un*bearable. Tonight the sidewalks in the Ginza are wet
from an afternoon rain and you're going from bar to bar,
getting as numb as you can, trying to drown out the sense of
a self that seems to have no place in the world. And then
at one of the upstairs bars your banker friend shows up,
the one you like, the married one you can't stop thinking about.
You sit with him and drink. You invite him back to your house.
Why should you care about propriety? The movie skips the part
with the two of you naked and sweating. It shows you waking up
beside the shallow indentation of his body in your sheets.
He's leaving town today, with his family, and when he sits
with you on the edge of the bed and takes your fingers
in his hand, you don't pull your hand away. You know where
this is going. His performance of love is sweet, but it won't
end well. Love, like thin air, is impossible to hold, and he's sorry,
he says, about the situation. Out of our control, he says. And after
he kisses your fingers you watch him stand, walk into the middle

distance, find his shirt on the back of a chair, tie his tie, slide his arms
into his coat, and the person you swore you would never become,
now you are that person. Because pride is the only thing you have
left, you keep your façade in place. Your role is to act with
decorum and strength, but now the veneer you've maintained
your whole life, you can feel it cracking, and by *it* I mean you.
If you could just jump, you think, from this life to another one,
you probably would. But where would you land? He doesn't
know that you're watching him as he slides an envelope under
the papers on your desk. It's probably money, possibly a lot,
but for you, there's only one thing to do. You pull your kimono
across your chest, walk him to the door, and when he's ready to go
you hug him one final time, slip the envelope back inside his
suit-coat pocket, and then, when you close the door, that's when
your body takes over, and you let it, finally, convulse
with the tears you've been dreaming about, tears
not of joy but they're yours.

When night descends on the Ginza,
although there seems to be nothing to live for,
in the movie you keep living. You've looked for
other jobs at other bars but the yen, they say,
has lost its value. Money, they say, is tight.
The daytime shops are shuttered for the night and
walking the wet sidewalks, you turn up the collar
of your coat. The autumn wind has a sting and
you think about the choices you have. Or have had.
But the choices anyone has get fewer and fewer and
it's not that you've wasted my life
searching for meaning, and now,
after a person has exhausted every possible way
of struggling with the world, with no help forthcoming,
with satisfaction inconceivable, the only option is . . .
there is no option. Just surrender. And

the reward for surrender is cessation, finally,
of hoping and trying, and when
after walking in spirals all night you arrive
at the stairway that leads to the club where you earn
your so-called living, you're clutching at your collar but
the worn fabric does nothing to shield you from the cold.
And if there's any indication of emotional liberation in your
posture, the camera doesn't show it. It shows only your feet
stepping up the carpeted stairs, the backs of your ankles
ascending, slowly, tread after tread and because
you've lost the sense of being what you used to be,
there's nothing I can do, she thinks, except
continue being what I am.

Bob Olen, *Marianne Moore throwing out first ball at Yankee Stadium season opener, 1968.*

Role Models

It is in small, everyday incidents, that the decision of how to live is made. It happens only if we are aware of what it is that we are about to do, or have done. Aye, there's the rub. It's not a matter of will or effort, but of love and attention toward what draws us and to which we respond—poetry, beauty, truth, or whatever—and respond not as to something separate from us but rather as to something with which we resonate.

That's a quote from my aunt, from one of the notebooks she kept during the last twenty years of her life. She was my father's older sister, a college professor and lifelong Quaker who, after she retired, wrote a book based on the letters of John Keats. She composed it on an early version of a personal computer, and by *book* I mean the pages she printed out, xeroxed, and bound inside a dark-green cover. She gave it to her friends and her teachers. She gave one to me, dedicated it to me and my father, and because she never married, never had any children, and because our affection for each other was meaningful for her, when she died I inherited her so-called papers. She left me the brittle plastic boxes that contained the notebooks she kept, the ones she used for writing about Keats, the ones that recorded her reactions to what she was reading, and other, more personal ones, charting the changes in her mind as she sought to address, in one way or another, what Keats called a "capability" but really it's desire, to live with "uncertainties, mysteries, doubts, without any irritable reaching after fact and reason." She'd been taught to valorize fact and reason, and her effort to transform herself into something more like Keats would only succeed if she could resist what she'd been taught, which meant resisting the part of herself that wanted everything known and settled and always about her.

The world is so much more exciting and beautiful—it comes into being if everything isn't just an extension of one's self.

Her given name was Harriet, but I called her Dot. She lived in a house by a canyon that bordered the college where she taught English literature. It was a modest bungalow with a bank of sliding glass doors that opened onto her deck, with orange trees in her backyard, and beyond them the canyon, and beyond that the mountains of what she called the *backcountry*. She had a dog for a while but mostly she lived alone, and when I would visit her we would sit on her deck, or in her patio, or in the two rattan swivel chairs she'd placed in front of her fireplace. I was young then, still developing a sense of self, still working out the roles I wanted to play in life, and mostly we talked about that, the process of becoming a person. She was doing it too, assessing the time she had left in life and trying to make the most of it. Part of our bond was the unspoken pact to discover who we would be if we had a choice. Her path led to a spirituality that hadn't been available to her when she grew up, and mine led to art and dance and writing plays, all aspects of what they call *expressing yourself*. As a young person, that's pretty much all I was interested in, my *self*, but I listened to her when she talked about books she'd read, and people she admired, and the memories that had affected her. I remember the way she decorated her house, with pieces of driftwood, a prayer rug she'd brought back from her travels, a black-and-white photograph of a desert ocotillo. Near her yellow telephone by the back door, on a small shelf, she'd made a display of postcards, views of nature and reproductions of paintings that must have inspired her.

In risking letting go of attachment, I open myself to the possibility of becoming a new creature. This liberation doesn't allow myself to repeat myself and doesn't give me a blueprint of what is to come—but is un-specified glory and of a different order from that of the senses.

Paintings usually have a story to tell, and in religious paintings it's often about a human being, standing under an azure sky, with mountains rising in the distance, and workers toiling in the valley, and the person in the foreground is about to become, not a new creature, but by recognizing the existence of something other than yourself, a transformation happens. It happens to the Virgin Mary in paintings depicting the Annunciation, when an angel appears and announces the fact that she has been chosen. It's not a moment of truth; it's not even a call to action. In the moment of the Annunciation a fact simply presents itself. *This is what is happening.* And for Mary, who's been preparing for this moment all her life, who's been reading her books and reciting her prayers, submitting to this higher authority isn't a decision. It's an honor. However, it's one thing to *study* God, another to experience the physicality of actual truth, of truth and beauty swooping down, like Zeus swooped down in the form of a swan, and in the Annunciation it's a beautiful angel announcing that God has chosen to enter you, to become you, and it's nothing you can prepare for.

The change that must take place is a change in my relationship to my self—to be free of any notions I have about myself, knowing that "I" am not my self.

Agnes Martin was about my aunt's age, an abstract artist whose paintings describe the presence of spirit. Her variously colored squares and rectangles seem to communicate with each other, attracting and repelling, and although the work is abstract, truth and joy were not abstract concepts to her. Like Georgia O'Keeffe she lived in New Mexico, alone in the desert, and like Dot she kept notes on what she was thinking and feeling, and although she suffered from schizophrenia, and maybe because she did, her paintings seem clear to me. Not clear as in *obvious*, but clear in the sense of being clean, being washed like you might wash an eyeball to let it see the world . . . and I was going to say *more clearly* but really it's *better*. Better to see without filters. Better to fare forward, even if you're unprepared for what you're faring into. Better to be something different, if that's what it takes to put joy in your life. Dot kept a book about Agnes Martin on her coffee table, a museum catalog that, like other books she cared about, she'd annotated, underlining passages she liked, scribbling in the margins, using the text like a guidebook, using Agnes Martin like I'm using *her*, to see how a person becomes something new.

Is it possible to see from a perspective other than our own? I think Keats could do it because of his capability for submitting to the absence of a personal identity.

In her book, *A Reading of the Letters of John Keats*, Dot quotes from the poem *Endymion*. "I leaped headlong into the Sea, and thereby have become better acquainted with the Soundings, the quicksands, and the rocks." Keats was a role model for her. He confronted what she, and what we all, at some point, try to confront: that which is painful and frightening. In his letters she found a courage she lacked, or thought she lacked, a courage she hoped might swoop down and guide her over the rocks and the quicksands, and the problem was, she'd been taught she wasn't worthy. She joked about what she called her *nearsightedness*, by which she meant her inability to see the interconnectedness of things, which was how God saw the world, which was what she wanted for herself. And although she blamed herself for getting in her own way, it's hard to make a headlong leap if you've been told you don't know *how* to leap. If you've been taught to feel unworthy, naturally you look around for something that *is* worthy, or worthi*er*.

For years I thought life was to be lived in relationship with an external world of things and people and events, and with rules I had been taught to conform to. Success and goodness were in relation to those things . . . Then one day a friend, who was something of a mystic, was laughing about people who thought that leading "a good and useful life" was all there was to living. Indignantly I protested. What other way was there? Her answer made no sense to me, and I pushed it away.

The friend my aunt mentions, *who was something of a mystic,* was a woman named Karena (pronounced ka-*rain*-ah). Although most of Dot's notebook entries concern her philosophical or spiritual questioning, the name Karena—or sometimes just K—keeps recurring. Karena was a woman Dot lived with in San Diego, and before that in Chiapas, in Mexico, where Karena had a finca. My other aunts never mentioned her, and my father rarely did, but Allen Ginsburg, who stayed at her finca, dedicated a poem to her. And for Dot, the mysticism she espoused must have been attractive. Attractive—because Karena was charismatic—but also frightening. She was inviting Dot to leap *headlong into the Sea,* and Dot wasn't used to leaping. Karena, according to a caption below her State College yearbook photo, was an actor, a performer in radio dramas, and she probably identified Dot as someone who might be devoted to her, someone she could teach. I imagine they slept in hammocks at the finca because Dot always had a hammock hanging in her patio in San Diego. Karena, who was younger, had a husband somewhere, and a daughter, but either she'd left them or they'd left her, and now she was free to pursue her spiritual life. And Dot, who yearned for that kind of freedom, was honored to tag along. By entering into a friendship with Karena she was taking a chance to exchange her own *little circumscribed existence* for something larger, for the promise of living, like Keats, without fixity or surety, and she was grateful that Karena, having rejected the old world, was letting her be part of a new one, a world Dot wanted to understand and love, and she didn't expect it to be easy.

When Saint Agatha discovered a new religion, based on love, she was brought before a tribunal, told to get down on her knees and disavow that love. Authority, in an effort to maintain authority, used intimidation, and Agatha was stripped of her clothes, thrown into a brothel, but instead of disavowing anything, she turned to her judges and tried to convert them. All her life she'd been taught that her body wasn't hers, that it belonged to someone else, and she didn't believe it. In paintings she's usually cast as a dark-haired Sicilian, sometimes a redhead, and whether her zealousness sprang from a sense of divinity, or from psychosis, nothing was going to stop her from believing in love. Like Dot, what she'd been taught seemed wrong to her, or limited, and she refused to let it change her belief. Changing that would have been like changing her mind, like literally substituting one brain for another, and *who I love and how I love is my decision.* In one of the paintings depicting her martyrdom she's strapped to a table in an ironmonger's workshop, torture devices hanging on the wall, her hands tied, and two men standing on either side of her are holding what look like gigantic wire cutters, each pincer biting down at the base of her nipples. One of the torturers glances up, expecting to see in her face the agony he's causing, but because she had her belief, and because she trusted her belief, the pain, so the story goes, only made her more devout.

Desire inevitably pitches one out of the present toward the future. One hangs from the future, over emptiness, by a fragile rope of longing and demand. Anxiety is inevitable, disappointment probable.

In spite of inevitable anxiety, Dot left the familiar life she knew to live with Karena, to begin a *vita nuova* in which the love she'd always kept to herself could finally be given away. Although she never thought of herself as courageous, when she told her mother that she was living with a woman in the jungles of Mexico, it couldn't have been easy. She didn't need to say she loved the woman; her mother already disapproved. Her mother, according to what I've heard, disapproved of almost everything. There's an apocryphal story about Dot when she was a girl, being driven home from school by her mother. The school was the Bishop's School, an Episcopal girls' school, and as I remember it, Dot is sitting in the back seat with a friend when her mother suddenly stops the car, turns around, and reprimands Dot for sitting too close to the friend. It's an apocryphal story because, according to my relatives, the friend in the back seat was a boy, but I imagine the scene with two girls back there, and there's no reason to sit apart from each other, so why is her mother telling her this? What is so wrong about what she's doing? Dot's feelings for Karena are not wrong, they're honest, and deep, and who gets to decide what's proper? Her mother had certain ideas about propriety, and found her daughter's attachment to this woman distasteful. But Dot was not a girl anymore. She'd left the place she started from and was venturing out, following Karena, looking at her circumscribed life and seeing the possibility of living a different, or bigger, or a purer life, and *for the first time,* she says, *I didn't feel guilty.*

I must feel open to myself if I am to communicate to another. I pick up the being of another as he does mine—and the body never lies. I can feel when I tighten up, or am too slack, and this feels like a letting myself down. My joy and sadness at this is irrelevant.

When Dot writes that *the body never lies,* I think it's because she felt her *own* body was a kind of sanctuary, a place where she could relax, where she didn't have to worry about making mistakes. *Fundamentally my nature is sound,* she said, *but I can violate its nature.* She used to joke that her mind was like a donkey, a capricious animal that acted dogmatically, contra naturam, or contra what was in Dot's own best interest. Trusting her body meant listening what her body was telling her, knowing that she might not understand, but she could try. That's what she wanted, to try as honestly as she could. Apparently, at Mills College, she was a pretty good athlete. In the 1920s she played tennis, doubles and singles, and later, watching tournaments on television she would marvel at how the players used their bodies, how the best ones were able to pick up the vibrations from . . . not an opponent across the net but a partner, like a dance partner. And it's possible, while she was studying in Madison, at the university, that she took dance classes. It would have been a way for her to understand her body, how it occupied space, and back then dance companies toured the Midwest, people like Doris Humphrey and Ruth St. Denis, and Dot was a little too early for Martha Graham, but anyone can be a role model, anyone who's come before, who's tried to do what you want to do, and even if their struggles were unsuccessful, or only partly successful, you can learn, by example, a way to be.

Like a lot of people her age, Dot admired the artist Georgia O'Keeffe. She was someone who'd come before, who dreamed of becoming a certain kind of person—in her case a painter—and set about doing it. She started by taking classes, training her eyes and hands, and when she saw she wasn't as good as she wanted to be, although she gave up her career for a while, she never gave up her ambition. And the question is: how did this unknown young woman suddenly transform herself into the Georgia O'Keeffe we recognize: independent, strong, living alone in her black dress, surrounded by the crags and endlessness of the desert? First of all, it probably wasn't sudden. She'd been working in New Mexico on her drawings and paintings, and one of them she sent to Alfred Stieglitz, who fell in love with it, and with her. During their time together, notably at Lake George, in New York, she let him take photographs of her hands. *My hands*, she said, *had always been admired*, and although the photographs are mainly focused on her hands, the subject is always her, a woman developing her stance, her way of being looked at, and part of it was the hands, and part of it was the way she looked at the photographer. Janet Malcolm called their relationship a collaboration, but because Stieglitz was twenty-three years older, an authority on art and art making,

Georgia eventually had to disentangle herself. Looking at her face, you can almost see her mind acknowledging the man behind the camera but looking beyond him, calculating the distance she had to go, and although he was using her to make his art, she was using *him*, using his eyes like a mirror to find the person she wanted to become.

I am very aware that it's only as I become a different kind of person that I can stop being critical and judging others—it's absolutely impossible to do it from your old way, from where you started.

According to the legend, Theodora Marković came to Paris to make a name for herself. And she started by changing *her* name, to Dora Maar. She studied art, searching for what she wanted to be and filling her life with people she wanted to know: Bataille, Brassai, and Jean Renoir. She was psychoanalyzed by Jacques Lacan, was friends with Man Ray and Lee Miller, and there are several versions of how she met Pablo Picasso. It might have been on the set of Renoir's movie, *Le Crime de Monsieur Lange*. Dora was the film's photographer. The more colorful version is set at Les Deux Magots, the bistro in Paris, famous as a hangout for artists and writers, and especially the friends of artists and writers. Dora was twenty-eight and Picasso was already a celebrity, the center of the room, and the story is almost too good to believe but apparently Dora, to be close to the center, sat at a table near Picasso's table. Picasso surrounded himself with friends and admirers, so his was a large table, and Dora at some point must have joined him because she took a penknife from her pocket and started stabbing the table. Not just the table; she'd placed her open palm on the tabletop, fingers spread, and as fast as she could she stabbed between her fingers, lifting the knife and bringing it down, and Picasso, apparently, was impressed. Apparently she'd been wearing black gloves, which she'd taken off to perform her trick, a trick which bloodied her hand, and probably that was the point. She wiped off the blood with one of the gloves and Picasso wanted the glove. He placed it in a vitrine, or so the story goes, and the story has all the drama and tempestuousness that make a good legend, and in it, Dora found the intensity she craved. She became Picasso's muse, *her* intensity inspiring him to paint her and draw her, and in photographs of them, taken by the sea in the South of France, Dora, wearing a two-piece bathing suit, standing on some beach rocks, a towel in her hand, is shaking her famously beautiful hair, getting the last of the water out of her ear, knowing that Picasso is watching her but refusing to let him distract her from the warm sun and the dry breeze, and the fulfillment of what must have felt like a dream.

While I am relating well to myself I am wholly unattached to any results or objectives. In that nonattachment lies my freedom and joy.

In all the boxes and folders and notebooks Dot left behind, I discovered only one photograph—a faded color snapshot of a woman, silhouetted by a window, sitting at Dot's kitchen table. Karena, holding a white ceramic cup, looks like any short-haired woman of indeterminate age. But the photo must have had significance for Dot because she saved it. Because Karena was possibly the love of her life. When she wrote about *a sense of oneness with God as I slugged for it when living with Karena*, she was talking about love, about a sense of connection that's *unattached to any results or objectives*, a feeling that takes you out of yourself and appears when you least expect it, when you're washing the dishes or hanging the clothes on the line. The expression *slugged for it* is a typical Dot expression. As is her use of the word *doing*, as in *I think the opposite of "doing" is love*. And how do you do the opposite of doing? That was her conundrum. How to move forward, toward an outcome, without becoming attached to that outcome. And if Keats was a model for her, a person who could live with uncertainty, she also had Karena, her mystic friend who made uncertainty real. Karena's conception of Dot didn't always align with Dot's conception of her*self*, but because she valued Karena's opinion, she tried to conform. She *slugged it out*, trying to feel a sense of connectedness, but how can you feel connected to someone who's dictating what form that connectedness should take? Dot didn't like her mother telling her what to think, and even if she found Karena's mysticism attractive, she had her own way, which wasn't Karena's way. But Karena was impatient. Come on, Harriet. I've been telling you about my vision of God but you seem so uncomprehending. And what could Dot say? Her idea of God was still forming. Karena was the mystic and she was more like Martha, the woman in the Bible who stays in the kitchen cooking for the more interesting people, like Jesus, and Mary, and Karena seemed like one of those people, someone who felt more strongly and believed more fervently, and *I grew up*, Dot wrote, *wanting to conform and to do well*. And in her effort to *do well* she constructed a role for herself as the student, and Karena was the teacher, and her job was to figure out what Karena wanted.

I think of Christ's "Love thy neighbor as thyself." Loving my neighbor doesn't consist of making him conform to what I find loveable, and so I suppose loving myself doesn't consist of changing myself into what I value.

In one of her notebooks, Dot wrote about feeling as if she was holding on to *a fragile rope of longing and demand*. She knows she's holding it, and she knows it's a worn-out rope that's about to snap, and why would anyone keep holding on to a rope like that unless that rope is all you have, the one thing preventing you from falling into despair, from plummeting down a narrow rock gorge into a raging river far below. Letting go of the rope would be crazy, crazy because it's counterintuitive, counterintuitive because you want to live. But that's what Keats was suggesting, what Karena was suggesting, and it's what Dot, in her book, was urging herself to do, to pry your fingers from the one thing holding you to the life you know and value. And that's the rub. It's hard to let go of what you value. Even when it's not very valuable. But Dot was willing to do it, ready and willing to let herself fall, not knowing where she might land, or if she would even survive, because she longed for a new kind of consciousness.

The sky and clouds I see outside, and the air between me and the cottage across the way, have fullness and substantiality because they are full of what I cannot see, the invisible.

Painting the Annunciation is theoretically impossible because, first of all, God is impossible to portray. The artist can depict the golden dove, shining its light on the Virgin, kneeling below a stained-glass window, holding a lily or reading a book or petting the fur of a dog, looking at the luminous robes of the angel hovering in front of her, but all it can show of the so-called announcement is the woman's *reaction* to the announcement, a reaction that, in some cases, seems ambivalent. In Botticelli's version of the scene, although Mary lets herself be looked at, she raises her hands as if defending herself, fending off the angel's invisible authority. In a painting by Gentileschi, the Virgin appears to grimace, as if she'd been punched in the belly, as if the pain of that sets off a chain reaction of grief and sadness that leads to a sense of powerlessness, a comprehension of what it means to be chosen, that someone *else* is doing the choosing, that her life, having been taken over, will no longer be hers. *All she is or ever hoped to be* she owes to the power that has somehow come to her, and although she'd been seeking it, in the moment of the actual announcement she feels alone. Soon the angel will be gone, the dog at her feet will have wandered away and the golden light from the Dove or from God won't matter. It's why she's sometimes shown reaching out to touch her prayer book, marking the passage she was reading, hoping she might, at the last minute, forestall the event and get back to her book but once the moment has started, although you theoretically have a choice, it's no longer yours.

The tendency [is] to let what you value turn into a fixity of thought and plan to which you then enslave yourself.

Dot attended a weekly service at the Quaker Meeting House in La Jolla. I went once, for my grandfather's funeral, and what happened was, everyone was quiet. They sat in rows, in a circle, eyes sometimes closed, speaking when the so-called spirit moved them. I remember sitting on the wooden bench, watching the faces across the circle, wondering when the spirit would appear in me, and move, and *how* it might move. What was the signal that let you know the impulse to speak came from God and not some conception or misconception or a desire to fit in.

Are my psychic patterns caused by a desire "to be taken care of"—e.g., with K? Although on one level I don't want to be taken care of, but to "take care of the other." Is taking care of another a projection of what you want done to you?

Marianne Moore was a poet, about Dot's age, who shuttered herself from the world, closeting herself and concealing herself, revealing her desires but only in poems, and then only obliquely. Which is why she often wrote about animals, creatures who, despite being creatures, had a humanity she could poetically embody. Writing about animals was a way to understand a self that was misunderstood, specifically by her mother, a woman she shared a bed with, who once wrote to her, "We are like people interrupted in love-making the minute any outside persons come in." Her mother, the first reader of the poems, often referred to Marianne as *he*, using the masculine pronoun when she wrote about her daughter's work. "I had to say that the poems he has worked on for months— for days unremittingly and speechlessly—were not just right yet." Marianne's father had gone, and her brother was close, but her mother's voice was the one she heard, the authoritative voice that told her what was good and acceptable, and sometimes, because they were *her* poems, she bridled at her mother's suggestions.

That's why her poetry, which is expressive, is also protective. Even the way she dressed, in the black cape and famous tricorn hat, was a way of creating a character she could hide behind, a character who was admired and lauded and invited to parties, a character who threw out the famous first pitch at a Yankees game, a character who, like Dot, never married, and who, unlike Dot, made art that people loved.

What is the hunger that I must not accede to? The hunger to feel better—seeing a panacea outside of myself. I must rather seek to understand why I feel bad—just look at it—instead of reaching out for relief.

When I used to sit with Dot on her backyard deck, under the large acacia tree, because I was young I was hungry for experience, hungry to know the facts of life. And by *facts* I mean what was tangible and visible, and Dot had developed a faith that something existed beneath those facts, a spirit that was hidden by appearances, but also resided inside those appearances. She was patient, willing to wait for that spirit to reveal itself, willing to forgo her demands for freedom and joy and happiness, and let those things appear on their own accord. But I was *impatient*. Freedom and joy meant *pursuing* freedom and joy, putting myself, not in the backseat but up in front, behind the steering wheel, doing the work that Dot had seemingly abdicated. Her willingness to passively wait for inspiration seemed, at the time, to be evidence not of virtue but of fear, that she was afraid that she didn't deserve the enlightenment she thought she wanted.

I wonder if my not getting really involved in anything—as with the League, or Friends, or the Sierra Club, or even reading—is part of my saying "no" to things, not giving myself to people.

Dot was on a tour of Japan, studying Buddhism with Alan Watts, when she received the letter from Karena. It was in her files, in an envelope addressed to Miss Harriet Haskell, Hiergan Hotel,

Kyoto. Written on translucent paper, it begins, "I must confess to having been distressed that I had hurt you so—even inadvertently." Someone has to care, if they're going to be hurt, and Dot obviously cared for Karena, and Karena knew she cared, and the letter goes on, "Beloved Harriet, it seemed to you as if there were a lack, something you were not admitted to, something that made you even more separated from a real relationship with me." In one of her journals Dot wrote, *What is it that happens when nothing takes place between two people, Ruth Brown and Charlie, and Karena and me?* I don't know who Ruth and Charlie were, but the expression *nothing takes place* sounds as if someone wanted something to take place and either Karena wasn't willing or Dot wasn't. "So many times," Karena says, "I opened my heart and my vision for you and received what seemed to me either dry bones or a caustic comment." She's writing a Dear Dot letter, ending the relationship, hoping Dot will see that it wasn't working, knowing she wouldn't, and she continues: "I am not trying to take the hurt away from you. That hurt was perhaps important and necessary for you [. . .] the one thing that would make you reject me more completely and therefore free yourself from me."

Anything that is the object of desire is in a sense unattainable. There will always be at least a membrane of separation. The very desire to overcome the separation prevents it, although the failure may tear the heart apart in longing.

Saint Lucy, the patron saint of the blind, is often depicted in a marketplace, standing on a tiled floor, surrounded by people who object to what she wants. Dot probably understood the desire to create a rampart against the voices that tell you what to do and how to love, and like Saint Lucy she tried to be honest. She tried to be brave and open and *stick to her guns* but at some point I think she was tired of constantly struggling, tired of trying to always be better or purer, and sometimes you just want to love, or hate, or cry if you have to. And maybe *that's* the rub. Lucy was not yet a saint when she found a love that gave her life meaning. And she refused to renounce it. And so she was sentenced to death. As she's being taken away to be sacrificed she prays, hoping for a miracle, and she becomes a saint when God intercedes, giving her the gift of being heavy. It's an odd gift, but by accepting it she becomes unmovable. The people surrounding her pull at her dress and tug at her wrists and legs, trying to move her in one direction, trying to tear her out of her spot and out of herself but God has made her like the heaviest metal imaginable, like cement, or like a rooted tree. And if that was the end of the story, it would have what they call a happy ending, but the story keeps going. In one of the paintings of her she's holding a silver tray in her hands, wearing a red dress, her long hair tied in a bun, her face looking up through the clouds toward heaven, and balanced on the tray are the two bloodied eyeballs taken from her face.

The problem with any story is, if it's fiction, because what happened never happened, the story isn't real. With nonfiction the problem is reversed. Because what happened *did* happen, it can't happen any other way. And because I think there's a place between the two, neither fiction nor fact, I'm drawn to movies. Although the events acted out by the characters aren't real, in the constantly moving images, as they happen, over and over, they *become* real, and the ending is always the same but the choices made to arrive at that ending seem like actual choices. In the 1928 movie about Joan of Arc, near the end of the film, when Joan, sentenced to die, faces her judges, all hardened, hate-filled men, because they seem to offer her a choice, she looks at them with the same trusting gaze she gives the rest of the world. Joan, as played by Renée Falconetti, doesn't ask, who gave you authority? Instead, she looks up at her judges, who are also her accusers, and she doesn't tell them to fuck off. Or if she does, because the film is silent, we don't hear it. We see her willingness to submit, deferring to the judges who have authority, an authority she's given them, and although we now know that authority corrupts, Joan didn't know it until, realizing that her belief was all she had, and refusing to separate herself from her experience of that, she got burned at the stake.

I observe that my "doing" has not responded to treatment. Is it that I can't change myself or even be changed?

Dot found, in Karena, someone with whom she could experience "in fearless yet in aching ignorance" what Keats had prepared her for, a person who would understand her, accept the love she had to give, and possibly return that love, and when you have a plan like that, and the plan doesn't go according to plan, when everything you've intended to do or say or love doesn't happen, doesn't come your way, and in fact seems to go the *opposite* way, passing you by, although you initially find the fault outside of yourself, you soon suspect that actually it's you, that maybe you haven't waited long enough, or transformed yourself completely enough, or honestly given yourself away.

I think God will wait until I have become a person. There are chances that I have missed. No doubt there are chances all around me that I don't see and take.

In one of her spiral notebooks Dot writes about *trimming a very long and high Eugenia hedge.* I remember the hedge. It grew between her house and what she called Doctor Love's yard. Dr. Love had been a dean at the college, someone Dot probably knew, and a wooden gate had been built into the hedge with a string that you pulled to open the gate. Dot had a birdbath on her side, with a statue of St. Francis, and the hedge was about twelve feet tall. She writes, *As I began working, it was as if I and each bit of the hedge I was about to cut were engaged in a cooperative adventure. I had no itch for finishing. There was no sense of hurry but rather of pleasure in the moment.* It's that *pleasure in the moment,* the sense of *cooperative adventure* must have encouraged Dot. It's what the Shakers were talking about when they spoke of making a place where God was welcome. And I think I've experienced moments like that, sometimes, when I'm writing, when the old cliché of the words writing themselves seems to happen. And when moments like that appear, you have to prepare yourself for the fact that they'll *disappear*. Because they will. And that's when the muscles in my neck start to tighten. It's barely noticeable, and not necessarily painful, but instead of feeling it, instead of noticing and accepting what's actually happening, I look for something to blame, something responsible for the feeling I don't want to be feeling. And that's the moment Dot describes when she's trimming her hedge. *As time passed, I tired, and saw how much still remained to be done, and everything changed. What I cut became an object, an enemy to be attacked with the clippers.* When she says, *and everything changed,* she's talking about desire turning against itself, obscuring what you want by making what you want an adversary.

How like me to demand for God to give me a mystic experience, and despair when he didn't. My relationship with Karena was another engulfment, my "vita nuova" a futile recognition of the need for something different but without real understanding.

Dot once told me that literature was the wrong profession for her. She preferred philosophy. Abstract ideas had meaning for her because she animated them with what she knew, what was meaningful for her. The book I'm writing now is a lot like the one she wrote about Keats. Keats and Hazlitt and Fanny Brawne were the role models that she quoted, and from their biographies she took the bits and pieces she could internalize and physicalize, and some of the stories in her book are cautionary, about Richard Nixon resigning, or her response to an out-of-control Eugenia hedge. In all of them she tried to find a coherence, a meaning that hadn't been fully arrived at, or settled, but she was on her way to getting it. And by meaning I mean love. Keats had found his, and she believed it was still here, still part of the world and waiting to be discovered. Her book is a record of her search. And if her writing was sometimes confused or clumsy or lost, sometimes I am too. That's why, for a long time, I put off reading her notebooks. Even the ones she'd provocatively labeled, *Private. Do not read.* Even when I started writing about her, I hesitated, partly because of the difficulty of deciphering her cryptic handwriting, but mainly because the words she wrote were written for herself. She never had the chance to read the book I dedicated to her—she died before I finished it—and the only reason I keep slugging away at *this* story is that *she* kept slugging away. I remember her patio, the green plate from Mexico on the stucco wall, me in the hammock and Dot in the folding aluminum chair with the yellow webbing. I remember her voice, the bend of her neck, the wrinkles at the side of her ears when she turned her eyes to meet mine, opening herself to whatever inchoate meaning I had to offer, offering her own in return. And although I can picture her face, the meaning that she gave me is hard to remember. This essay, which is partly an homage to her, an expression of the love I felt, and feel, can't help misrepresenting the spirit she embodied, a spirit she tried to understand and express and now it's gone.

I long for a way of becoming grown without confrontation, without meeting the adversary—myself.

When Dora Maar was abandoned by Picasso, although she probably had something to say about it, it didn't influence the event. He gave her some paintings, a house on a hill, and when the *fact* of the breakup sank in, the fact that the life she'd desired and valued had been taken away, that she was alone, she tried adjusting. She couldn't just abandon her old intensity, so she tried to find a semblance of it by visiting the old bars and seeing old friends but that didn't help. And drinking didn't help. She fell into something like depression. People who knew her knew it was serious; a doctor prescribed electroshock therapy to shake out what was stuck in her, or knotted up in her. And that, or the psychoanalysis, seemed to work. She understood that she could never replicate the privilege and passion she'd known with Picasso, but now she could have a different passion. She was older, still driven to find meaning in her life, and her search for meaning led her, after a while, to Buddhism, which helped by giving her a sense that the life she was living was not as real, therefore not as painful, as it seemed. She was interested in a variety of spiritual paths but the one she eventually came back to was the old Roman Catholicism of her youth, a youth she'd lost by the time she said, "after Picasso, only God."

Is the answer to accept that I can't change myself? And try to get in a state so that God can do it? I have a feeling that God has tried.

In her notebooks, along with references to Karena and God, Dot makes references to Ace. Ace was her dog. Part collie, part husky, he'd been my family's dog, and when I went away to college Dot inherited him. I said before that Karena was the love of her life, but I'd forgotten about Ace. In renaissance paintings dogs symbolize loyalty, and in the case of Ace the loyalty went both ways. She writes about *his eagerness and his good will*, and because I was away at college I don't know the facts surrounding his death, but what she wrote about him seems closer to love than anything she wrote about Karena. She talks about the *vividness with which I can see Ace, feel his hair, anticipate his movements—and the fact that never, never will I see or touch him again.* When she writes about *the reality of the impossible absence,* although she doesn't use the word love, she seems to know what she's lost. *How quickly and completely in a minute or two he eased down on the table and was gone. And when I took off the paper that the vet had put over him, and when he was in his grave, how at peace his dear face looked.* Ace, apparently, had been failing. His eyes had become cloudy, and being half blind he was stumbling, confused about where he was, and who Dot was, and *I am sure he knows I meant the best in wanting to relieve him of his weakness.* When she says *weakness* she means what the pain was doing to him, and because she loved him she decided to put him down. That's what we call it when an animal is killed, and when the animal is loved, how can you talk about it? *I hope I was not pushed by my own distress. Was this the same impatience that made me refuse to accept something less with Karena—I must learn to be patient with what life brings. And I must learn not to be driven to take action and settle something—I must let things unfold without imposing my will on them.* Dot was writing to understand what she was feeling, and she wrote, *Now, a week later, I feel real grief and miss him terribly. There is a great emptiness in the absence of someone to whom I responded. I feel very alone.*

The being left out is of course an old feeling.

Dot felt freest, I think, when she was working in her garden, out in the open air, wearing her old work clothes, raking leaves or gathering oranges from her backyard trees. She used an old wooden pruning tool to cut off the fruit which she would then squeeze by hand into the orange juice we would later drink together. She encouraged me to join her in the garden, to get down on my knees beside her, digging holes in the soil and mixing in the compost. That's how we bonded, how *she* bonded with me, by working with me, and it started when I was five or six and she would let me help her fill a burlap sack with *leaf mold*, one of us holding the sack and one of us shoveling in the decomposing layer of leaves. That was the kind of work she loved, physical and tactile, and although we occasionally talked while we worked, mostly we did our jobs in silence, side by side, thinking our separate thoughts. I didn't pay much attention, then, to the way she used her body, to the graceful way she worked, placing boulders in a tree pit or making tapioca at her tan Formica countertop. I was young, and she was another generation, a mentor or advisor or confidante who wanted me to like what she liked, who invited me to hike in the Cuyamaca hills, who encouraged me to see the world that she saw and to appreciate it the way she did. As I got older, and as she got closer to the end of her life, I noticed her doing that less and less. She became less pro-scriptive, allowing me to become more and more what I was slowly, awkwardly becoming. And it wasn't that she didn't care. In a way, she cared more. During a period of my life when I was stuck, con-fused about what I was supposed to be doing, she let me use her house to experiment with performing hypnosis on people who an-swered my newspaper ad. She must have seen that I was lost, and she probably felt she could've fixed what was wrong in me, make it better, but she let that go. And that's when she wrote her book.

Yesterday, as I was running off pages on my printer, I was looking through the window at hummingbirds and bumblebees buzzing about the red flowers on the large bottlebrush in front of the window. I real-ized that I was looking at them as Keats had looked . . . delighting in their going about the activities of their living in a world emptied of my personal self.

After the stroke paralyzed the left side of my aunt's body, although she continued to make entries in her notebooks, she decided to move herself to a nursing home, a nursing *facility* they called it. It wasn't the life she'd wanted, but *Aging requires adjusting to and los-ing gradually the capability of doing what had constituted your living and your idea of your self.* She'd been assigned one of the cottag-es, and after her stroke I remember sitting with her on her rattan chairs in front of a large window, looking out to the trees outside, and the stroke made talking difficult but she tried. She seemed to appreciate the opportunity to notice her mouth, how the muscles and nerves made it work, how her tongue, although not seeming to cooperate, was willing to cooperate if she was. In one of her last notebooks she wrote, *Quite soon I had a compelling realization that in this new and strange environment no one was going to take responsibility for me, I had to do that myself. This wasn't an idea, a concept, but quite exactly a realization which included such things as figuring out how to get my clothes marked with my name before they went to the wash. This responsibility was a springboard of focus and strength. It motivated me and awakened observation and ingenuity. It lighted some sort of living wick.*

Elliott Erwitt, *Sophia Loren and Anthony Perkins on the set of* Five Miles to Midnight, Paris, 1962.

Five Miles High

Sophia Loren and Anthony Perkins were movie stars who, in 1962, played characters in a movie called *Five Miles to Midnight*. Sophia plays an Italian newlywed living in Paris, and Tony is her boyish, seemingly innocent husband. The story begins one night when Sophia tells Tony she wants a divorce. Tony Perkins, who made *Psycho* a few years earlier, carries from *that* film a slightly demented aspect, a maniacal persona he'd worked out for Norman Bates and now, hearing the news that Sophia no longer loves him, he refuses to accept it. That's why I say he's *seemingly* innocent. Later, when she reiterates her desire for autonomy he slaps her cheek, lashing out like a spoiled child deprived of what it cannot have. And although he later apologizes, there's no remorse in his boyish face. Whatever he wants, he expects it to be given to him, and he'd slap her forever if he thought it would soothe him or heal his psychic wound. Like a character in Greek tragedy, or like the character in *Psycho*, he's nice enough on the outside, but if you scratch the surface, which Sophia did by marrying him, a different person emerges, which is why her body recoils whenever he's in the room. And he's often in the room. And being narcissistic, he's very aware of her body's reaction to him, the way it stiffens, and tenses, and what drives him crazy is not the fact that she doesn't love him. What drives him crazy is that she's *chosen* not to love him. She's unwilling to participate in the performance they began together but now she's done with it. She *wants* to be done with it. And at the airport, after he buys insurance and boards a plane, after she waves goodbye from the tarmac and the plane takes off, with him temporarily out of her life she goes back to the empty apartment and she lets herself feel what it feels like to step out of a cage. She lets go of what she's been holding, which is him, in her body, the oppression of that. The tension that used to grip the muscles of her neck and chest and shoulder blades starts to loosen. Her hip bones swivel in their sockets. Then she hears a news flash on the radio. A plane that was going to Casablanca crashed in the sea with no survivors. Tony was going to Casablanca. Tony was on that plane. And now Sophia is skipping around the small apartment, not completely happy but experimenting with happiness, rearranging pillows on the sofa, having a smoke, going to work the next day and meeting a man. And imagine the next scene, when she's sorting her mail, looking for a letter that will certify her freedom. She hears a rattling at the kitchen door. She opens the door and it's Tony, limping, his face bloody. And we're meant to believe that, although everyone else on the airplane died, he didn't. But because the authorities *think* he's dead, he comes up with a plan. He'll *pretend* to be dead. To collect the insurance money. But to do that he needs her. He needs her to negotiate with the world, to be his go-between, and even if she doesn't like his plan, and even if she doesn't like *him*, because she wants to be *done* with him she agrees to be part of the lie.

If you base your life on the dream of being in love, when you find someone who seems to fulfill that dream, you tend not to look too closely at what you've found. You get up in the morning and like any morning you get out of bed. You glance back as you walk to the kitchen, and there's the person you love, still under the covers, and you make some toast. A crystal you bought years ago from a junk store hangs in the window, refracting the morning sunlight. You bring coffee and toast to the bed on a breakfast tray and the person sits up. He's sleepy, naked, his hair delightfully tousled. You think it's delightful, and that *he* is delightful, and because your history together is just beginning, because you're still giddy from the chemicals of love, you're happy to cut the bread and toast the bread and spread the butter. And when you join him under the covers, lying back against the shared pillows, the tray on your common lap, you're willing to let contentment have a place in your life. You drink your cup of coffee, read aloud a poem you wrote, and the person declares his love to be like Dante's love for Beatrice, worshipful, classical, and you imagine him gazing at you as you read, admiring the way your skin moves miraculously from your cheek to your chin to your neck, and maybe he is. But also, he must be thinking about the bread in the kitchen because he interrupts your reading to mention the fact that he wouldn't mind very much if you brought him another piece of toast. He may even kiss you just before he says it, or just after, and because you recently made love you don't mind getting out of bed, walking across the wooden floor, stepping into the small yellow kitchen, cutting a slice from the loaf of bread and dropping it in the toaster. You've been told all your life that the feeling of love, and especially of being *in* love, is compensation enough for buttering toast and spreading honey and even cleaning the house, a job he's less than scrupulous about. And you're right if you think your role models are slightly outdated. But that's what you have to work with. And that's how it happens. In the beginning you're young, not paying attention, thinking, I'll never be bored or stuck or desperate, and because that's how you think, when you see him throw off the covers and sit on the edge of the bed, arching his back, brushing his fingertips through his hair, you see an idealized image of love, caught mid-gesture, like a single frame in a larger film that you hold in your mind, preserving it, adoring it, and because you're afraid of losing the image if you look too closely, you don't really notice the dirty dishes on the breakfast tray, rising and falling as your belly rises and falls, and the tray, which had once been on your common lap, is now on your lap only.

In the movie, Tony tricks Sophia into being his accomplice. She's the only one who knows he isn't dead, that he's only pretending to be dead, and to ensure her cooperation he lies to her, tells her he'll leave her alone the minute he collects the insurance money. But that seems to be a long time coming. And in the meantime he's constantly underfoot, keeping track of where she goes and who she sees, reading her mail, listening in on her phone conversations like a spoiled child. And like a spoiled child the words coming out of his mouth are bitter and venomous. And that's why she's desperate to leave him. And sensing that, he becomes cloying, suspicious, demanding she perform the role he's given her, which makes her more desperate. Which makes him want to hold her down or tie her down, and they go back and forth like that, or around and around, and the only thing that keeps her from running away is the thought that soon it will be over, that eventually *he* will be over. But he's not. Like a creature from Dante's hell, he keeps returning, circling back, and the problem is: it's *her* hell. And it's driving her crazy. The camera follows them around the small apartment, him following her from bathroom to bedroom and he won't even give her a chance to stand by herself on the balcony. She has no place to breathe. She literally can't get the air she needs to fill her lungs and in English the movie's title is *Five Miles to Midnight* but in France it has a different title, and every time she thinks she might have gotten free of him the same thing happens, over and over, and the title makes sense: *Knife in the wound.*

The definition of *mithridatism* is the gradual inoculation against the effects of poison, or the ability to tolerate something harmful. The term comes from the legendary king Mithridates, and one of the legends told about him is about his photographic memory. When he addressed his thousands of troops he addressed every single soldier by name. Another legend concerns his fear of being poisoned. To protect himself against the outcome of a prophesy, he began taking tiny doses of every poison he could get his hands on, gradually increasing the dosage to inoculate himself, hoping to tolerate an amount of poison that would normally be lethal. Apparently he would demonstrate his newfound power by standing on a dais in front of his people and ingesting compounds like hemlock and cyanide and mandrake. And surviving. But at one point, in the middle of a battle, about to lose the battle, rather than be captured by enemy soldiers and taken prisoner, he decided to kill himself. He had enough poison on hand, but his poison-taking regimen had inured him to the effects of the poison, and the only option he had if he wanted to get out of the life he was caught in the middle of, was to kill himself by falling on his sword.

Sophia Loren was in her late twenties when she made *Five Miles to Midnight*. She'd probably been in love, knew what it was to fall *out* of love, and the movie documents the disintegration of her relation-ship with Tony. In the movie she thinks, *if I can just be free of it, if I can shake it off or cough it up*, and the *it* is him, but how do you expel what's already part of you. We see her in a black sweater, her dark hair under a silk scarf, sitting behind the wheel of a getaway car. She watches Tony in the rearview mirror, getting bigger and bigger as he walks up the sidewalk, carrying a suitcase filled with money, the insurance payout, and like a person trying not to be nervous, he slides into the passenger seat of the old Peugeot or Citroën and he tells Sophia to drive. And she does. She thinks she's taking him to a railway station or a bus depot but he tells her to keep driving, through the streets of Paris, through a suburb of Paris, past plane trees and gray skies and like a person who *is* nervous, when she sees an accident up ahead she thinks it has something to do with her. A bicyclist has been knocked to the cobblestones and bystanders are running toward the rider, who's wounded, possibly bleeding, and Sophia imagines a chance to open the door and exit the car, stepping out onto the cobblestone street and running through the crowd of people, through a marketplace filled with cabbages and vegetables and not looking back, disappearing into the unknown bodies, her scapulae turning into wings, spreading like wings and flying her away but Tony, coiled up in his seat like an animal—half badger, half weasel—grabs her wrist. He tells her, *keep driving*. He doesn't tell her, *look away*, but we see her face *turning* away from the freedom she'd imagined and following his directions, internalizing his directions, and maybe, she thinks, it's not that bad. Maybe I can stand this, at least for a while. Her thoughts become a kind of analgesic, allowing her a chance to take a breath, to come up for air, but the way Sophia plays the scene there *is* no air, or it's too thin, or there's an obstruction in her lungs. Tony has decided that it's better if she stays with him. I've grown attached to you, he says, and it's true that something has grown. Like a virus. Having found a host, it attaches itself to her, feeding on her, and to free herself she proposes a deal. You take the money. I won't turn you in. Just please let me go. That's her deal, but the deal falls through because, first of all, Tony enjoys the power he has over another human being, the dominance, the authority, plus he enjoys her suffering. He finds it physically pleasurable. And because he has no intention of forgoing that pleasure, even if she could sit him down and reason with him, like the character in *Psycho*, he'd be unreasonable. Because his *desires* are unreasonable. And when he casually announces that she'll be coming with him to Belgium, what can she say? What she can *do* is inoculate herself. That's why she swallows the poison. It's metaphorical at first, and she does it almost unwittingly. A thought comes into her head, not even fully formed, just the tone of a thought, and then another one comes, and then one after that, and each of her thoughts is a tiny dose, like a single frame in a larger film. And when she looks at the sky in front of her, at the stars in the sky, or the clouds that are blocking the stars, the poison she's taking, she feels it working, finding a home inside her body, and maybe it isn't a poison.

When I was in my twenties people often told me, you look like Anthony Perkins. It happened almost weekly. I was thin, *gangly* you might say. I worked at a theater where people knew about old movies, were familiar with actors and actresses from the past. Sometimes, seeing the resemblance, they would refer to me not as Tony, but as *that intense guy*, or that *crazy guy* from *Psycho*. Perkins is famous, primarily, for the role of Norman Bates, but he played other offbeat characters. And by offbeat I mean literally not quite in sync with the normal rhythm. In one movie he played a slightly manic baseball player who undergoes electroconvulsive therapy. In *The Trial*, by Orson Welles, he was also manic, a Kafka stand-in driven crazy by what he couldn't control. In 1958 he starred with Sophia Loren in *Desire Under the Elms*, a version of *Hyppolytus*, by Euripides, about a newly married queen who falls in love with her husband's son, played by Tony. He often played conflicted, dissatisfied young men whose dissatisfaction expressed itself in his body, in his posture and gait, and although I didn't think of myself as dissatisfied, once I was told by a South American poet that I looked fearful. *Fear Strikes Out* is the name of the movie in which Tony was given the electric shock. Whether it was fear, or anxiety, or the pressure of constantly hearing about the physical correspondence between me and this persona best known for matricide, I sometimes pretended to stab the air like Tony did in the shower scene in *Psycho*, as a joke, a way of deflecting the effect of constantly reminding people of someone they didn't even know except to know he was psychotic. And it was gradual, but after a while my resemblance to Tony began to feel like a weight, like an extra body I carried around on my back, influencing my movements and directing my movements, and was heavy. And I was ready to jettison the heavy weight, but how could I jettison what I couldn't even separate from myself.

Sophia, driving through the flat, dimensionless night, is trying to control what's driving her crazy by focusing on driving, watching the headlights of the car illuminate not farms or towns but only the fog in front of her. Tony, curled up in the passenger seat, leaning against the passenger door, is trying not to fall asleep but it's late, he's been under a lot of stress, and sometimes he can't stop his eyelids from closing. He doesn't see the road they're on, or the signs on the road for *deviation*, which is French for *detour*, and she follows the directions, following the other cars, taking the first detour, then the second, and then we see a close-up of her face, the windshield wipers swinging back and forth in front of her, and watching her face you can almost see her thoughts as they cross the muscles of her forehead, crossing her eyes as if crossing her mind, each thought altering the thought that came before, enlarging it, compounding it, and if we could slow down her thoughts and see them individually we would see the gradual mutation of love. She's habituating herself to ideas that had once seemed unthinkable and now seem, not quite normal, but possible, even necessary, and anyway it's too late. Every so often she glances across to the passenger seat and there's Tony, asleep, his hair falling over his forehead, occasionally looking up, seeing if they're on the right road, and then closing his eyes. They're supposed to arrive at the border at midnight, the *frontier* in French, and the *deviation* signs on the road are getting more frequent. Sophia can't be sure if he's really asleep, or just pretending. Waiting to catch her. He always seems to be catching her, *in the act*, and she's tired of acting, tired of performing a role that doesn't exist. *Just breathe*, she thinks, and she lets her ribs become like a bellows, letting oxygen fill up the cells in her chest. And to say she *smelled her freedom* would be overly poetic, but what she used to think she needed, now her dependence on that, her attraction to that, has waned. But how can I separate myself from what I used to be? That's her question, and the title is *Knife in the wound* because knives are good at cutting things out, cutting things off, and because *what I used to be* is part of the past, she believes she can excise that part of her and still survive. She can tolerate whatever poison she has to take because she's already taken the antidote. And whether the *wound* is hers or the *knife* is hers, as the antidote gets stronger and more potent she gets more and more used to her new condition, which is more and more separated from Tony, and when the idea of living without him gets strong enough, or necessary enough, when she feels it leaking into the area around her diaphragm, expanding and contracting, the next *deviation* sign appears. And although the arrow on the sign clearly points to the right, she turns to the left, leaving the well-worn highway and the cars on the highway and now she's driving on a one-lane road, completely deserted, no other lights because no other soul is in evidence. I don't remember what song was playing on the soundtrack. A xylophone I think, following them, into the night, and she sees up ahead a sign for the Belgian border, five kilometers away. The gears make a whining sound when she downshifts, slowing down and pulling to a stop near an old stone wall. She's been driving for hours and when Tony wakes up she tells him the car has a flat. He rubs his eyes as you'd rub your eyes to wake them up, and he says he'll take a look. For some reason he rolls down his window. He brushes his hand through his hair and his movements seem almost robotic. He opens the door, steps out of the car, and when he sees the sign for the border he makes a comment. Almost midnight, he says, and he squats down to examine the tire. And the car at that point starts backing up. We see him watching as it moves in reverse. Her plan all along? To leave his desperate, distorted world and drive to another world, without him? But there's still the *wound*. The wound is her inability to extricate herself from a situation that confuses her and gnaws at her and because that situation is Tony, the only way to change it is to end it, to kill it, to put the car in gear, put her foot on the gas, and it doesn't register to him what's happening. He looks up, caught in the headlights, caught in the middle of whatever gesture he was performing, elbows bent, arms akimbo, dancing a dance from another time, the *twist* or the *frug*, and *Honey?* He's half standing, his head tilted, his hands not quite shielding his eyes from the beam of the headlights, and *Honey?* He calls her Honey. He still has a trace of the gangly môtelier he played in *Psycho*, still a little crazy, a little fey, a little Frankenstein-like as he waves to her as if saying hello. And then the car knocks him over, knocking his body into the dirt. And then she backs up, the car bumping over his body, crushing it, his twisted arm raised like a creature from a dark lagoon. And then she comes at him again, the tires of the small sedan breaking his already broken bones, and because the sedan is small she backs up and does it again, and again, forward and back, his body still writhing like a worm in the mud, crushed like a worm and Sophia doesn't look away. That's why she took the poison. To be able to be done with him. To be able to change her reaction to him, her attachment to him, and her memory of that attachment. And although it worked, it couldn't work completely because her attachment was only a symptom. The thing she was trying to change was love itself.

Roberto Rossellini, still from *Germany Year Zero*, 1948.

Year Zero

In the movie my name is Edmund. I'm about thirteen, fourteen at the most, and I say *in the movie* because, although the story is about me, it's not mine. It's set in Berlin, after the war, the city in rubble, and people waiting in lines for food. Food doesn't exist, but lines exist because hope still exists, and the movie is about that hope, about the possibility of not just surviving your situation but changing it. By changing who you are. That's why I'm waiting in line. People have died during the war and digging their graves is a job, which is scarce, and when I finally get to the front of the line the man with the ration book looks at me, at my skinny arms, my smooth face, and he knows right away I'm not sixteen. You're supposed to be sixteen to work at a job, so I lie. And I guess he believes the lie because he holds out a shovel. This is what I've been waiting for, a chance to help myself and my family and when I reach out to take the shovel's handle, right about as I get my fingers around its grip, he yanks it from my hand. He passes it to the man in line behind me. You're a girl, he tells me, meaning I'm not strong enough, or old enough, and that's what I mean when I say the story isn't my story. If it was my story I would be stronger and older, I would take the shovel and take control, and that's why stories frustrate me: the constraint. Watching a movie over and over, after seeing the choices a character has, and the scarcity of those choices, sometimes you want to change the story.

The dilemma of the movie is: without an identification card you can't work. And without work you're lost. And because a person wants *not* to be lost, when Edmund sees a piece of paper in the dirt, thinking it might have value, he picks it up. It's an identification card, tied to a length of string, and he ties the string like a necklace around his neck. When he goes back to the foreman, by showing the card, he's saying, basically, *I am legitimate*, and the foreman passes him a shovel, points to a hole in the ground. And this is how stories change. They come to an obstacle, a bump in the road, a detail that has to be altered or tweaked, and even something insignificant, like a thought, if you alter its shape you get some elbow room in which you can begin to play the part you've been wanting to play. And any part is a start. One part leads to another, and Edmund begins chipping away at the hard earth, shoveling dirt to earn the coupons to buy the food, and everyone needs food, including the people waiting in line who think that, by working, you're taking from them what they desperately need, their food, and when they complain to the foreman he grabs you by the string around your neck and he pulls you away, taking the shovel out of your hands, and by extension, taking the story out of your hands.

In the story, I'm following a group of kids. My brown portfolio bag is strapped like a rucksack to my shoulders and we're following a horse-drawn coal cart. I'm scooping up pieces of coal that fall on the ground, filling my bag because coal means heat, and there's never enough for my father and brother and now we'll be able to cook our food. I cross a cobblestone platz, once busy with bicycles and streetcars and now, near the river, a small crowd has massed together, pulled as if magnetically, and I'm pulled too, not wanting to miss what they're all trying to glimpse, what they're all reaching out for. A horse, lying on its side, in the street, is writhing, not yet dead but lifting its neck, struggling like Nietzsche's horse to extricate itself from the situation. I can't see what the people are doing to the horse but some of them have knives, and the cry of the horse is audible in my body. I say *in my body* because I feel a pain in the fibers of my flesh, resonating under my skin, in my organs and blood and Nietzsche, at the time, was living in Torino, in Italy, and he also felt the cries. He walked to the horse that was lying in the dirt, a horse who'd refused to pull its cart, was too exhausted to pull, and apparently the owner of the horse started whipping it. The townspeople had formed a circle around the horse and Nietzsche, attuned to pain and cries of pain, pushed the crowd aside and when he stepped into the circle, letting the whip beat against him instead of the horse, holding the horse by its long neck, protecting the beast who like him was suffering, that's when some people say he went mad. And maybe that's what I should have done.

Germany Year Zero was a movie made in 1948, in ruined Berlin. In it, a boy named Edmund lives with his father and brother and sister in what, before the war, was a single-family apartment but now it's divided, the rooms occupied by several families, all using the same bathroom. The landlord, the man whose apartment had been requisitioned, resents the other families, and especially Edmund's father, who was anti-Nazi during the war, and although everyone is anti-Nazi after the war, the landlord is *less* anti-Nazi. And because Edmund's father is sick, the family uses more gas, and more electricity, and they try to pay their share but it's difficult. The landlord calls them spongers, threatens to have them evicted. He blames them for his troubles, and that's what can happen when there isn't enough, enough light and gas and really it's life, Edmund's life, taking up the space the landlord wants for *his* life, for *his* family. But also, he wants to seem reasonable. He wants to present himself as fair and compassionate and one day he gives Edmund an errand to run. Simple, he says. He'll pay me to take a scale (he'd been a butcher before the war) and sell it on the black market for three hundred marks. That's the amount he wants. It's worth much more, he says, and Edmund thinks, great. This is the opportunity I need.

Edmund's sister worked at night to keep the family together. There weren't many jobs for women, and *working* meant going at night to a jazz club, dancing with men and drinking with them, looking nice, barely sipping her drink so she wouldn't get drunk, and when cigarettes were offered, instead of smoking them she saved them and sold them later. That's how she kept us together. When men, even nice men, even without the implied promise of sexual favors, wanted to talk she would listen, and talk was fine but there was always the inequality of the transaction. All transactions are about commerce, which is someone selling something to someone else, and the conversations my sister was selling weren't worth as much as what other girls were selling, younger girls, and she couldn't compete. And anyway, she had a boyfriend. That's what she told us. And I think she believed it, believed he was still being held in a camp or a jail and would soon be released, but probably not. Probably he was dead. And she must have known he was dead but she had to believe her story. If she didn't believe it she'd be lost, and no one wants to be lost, I don't, but what if the story you're in is not the right story?

In the story, I carried the butcher's scale like a baby, down the stairs and out to the street. I knew where people sold things, along the central Strasse and I set the scale on the curb and started waiting, looking for buyers, trying to catch the eyes of passersby. But because money was scarce, no one was buying. But I had a job, to sell, and I wasn't going to quit until I had the three hundred marks. And that's when two men drove up in a small brown truck. They parked, got out, and the driver walked to the scale and lifted it, examining it, gauging its weight and pretending to test its worth and finally announcing to me, this is junk. Worth nothing. He carried the scale to the back of his truck while the other man, a bigger man, stood between me and the thing that was mine, or had been mine, had been entrusted to me and now, when the driver sat in the seat behind the steering wheel, I told him I wanted my money. Maybe a box of money was under the seat and he was going to open it and give me what he owed me. That's what I was hoping. But hoping is passive. I wanted *not* to be passive. I didn't care if the men were bigger than I was. And when the man tried to close the driver's-side door, I stepped in front of it, preventing it from closing, preventing the man from taking my scale and my money and with it my story, making it *his* story. I must have pleaded with him to pay my price but he pushed me away, closed the door, and when he locked the door I hit my fist against the window. I didn't care if I broke the glass. I was crying, I think, at this point, and when the man rolled down the window he looked out at me with his blue eyes and he said, you want money? And pretending to be reasonable he held out two metal cans, potted meat, probably rotten, and yes, I wanted to be paid, and the man dropped the cans out the window and the truck drove off and that's the helplessness that Edmund can't stand.

Who knows what potted meat is worth. Possibly a lot. Probably not. I probably know it's worthless when I climb the stairs and there's the landlord at the landing, waiting for his money. When I hold out the metal cans of meat I know what they mean when they say *hope against hope*. The landlord slaps them out of my hands. They roll across the floor and under a chair. You worthless little shit. He grabs my ear and reaches into the pockets of my shorts, checking my portfolio bag, pulling on my ear but I don't have his money. And when I tell him what happened, how the men in the truck left nothing except the two tin cans, even if he believes me he refuses to believe me. In my story I'm good, *trying* to be good, and in his story, if I even exist, I'm an obstacle. In his story I'm a liar. I'm stupid and dishonest and the fact that I did my best doesn't matter because my best is shit. I'm not fit. That's what he says. It's survival of the fittest. If this was a jungle you'd be put out to die, which is what you should be, you and your whole entire family. And although I know it's a movie, and the movie is just one version of my story, because I'm *in* the movie, it's hard not to think that I ought to be punished.

One afternoon I find myself wandering into the Russian sector. It was a no-man's-land, a once-nice neighborhood with wrought iron fences and empty mansions, and standing near a gate, wearing a sort of Bavarian hat, Mr. Henning was waving to me. He'd been my history teacher, and now he was talking to a boy who'd been at my school, an older boy, and Mr. Henning was smoothing the boy's blond hair. National Socialism was now against the law but Mr. Henning didn't seem to care. When the boy left, he invited me into his mansion. It wasn't his. He rented a room from a friend, and because he'd been a teacher, and because a teacher's job is to guide young minds, I asked him how you're supposed to be good in a world that seems to have no place for goodness. His room was on the second floor, with a bed, a large window, and I remember one time in Seattle, on a vacation with my family, waiting for the boat that would take us up the Puget Sound and I'd gone off exploring, in a forest. Being Seattle, it was a rain forest, something unknown to me. I was kneeling beside a rotten log when a man appeared. I don't remember his face but I remember his khaki pants, and I remember him asking me if I wanted to touch his penis. I don't re-member him taking it out, and I don't remember thinking he was a pervert because, like Edmund, I had no concept of what perversion was. I remember telling him I didn't want to, and he seemed to accept that, and maybe Mr. Henning wasn't a pervert, just fond of young people. Whatever he was, he had a job for me, and I wanted a job because a job was a way to take action, a role I could play and I needed a role, and Mr. Henning was offering me that opportuni-ty. But don't tell anyone, that was his stipulation, and the question of goodness comes up because, if what he was proposing was good, then why should I keep it a secret? But I let that question go. Like a good dog I was eager to fetch what the master dangled in front of me, just out of reach, and if I had to adjust my idea of what good-ness was in exchange for his treat, I was willing to do that. I was young, still forming ideas of right and wrong and the difference be-tween my brother, a Nazi, and my father, an anti-Nazi, seemed not to be so great. Mr. Henning put his hand on my shoulder and said, I hope I can trust you, intimating that he *wanted* to trust me but maybe he shouldn't, maybe I wasn't ready, and I had to show him I was, that I was old enough and responsible enough and willing to be whatever was necessary to become myself.

Become yourself. That's what Krishna told Arjuna on the field of battle in the Indian epic, the *Mahabharata*. Arjuna was a king who found himself without a kingdom. He was the pupil of Krishna, the god, and at one point in the story he finds himself on a field of battle faced with two options, neither desirable: Do nothing to stop his half-brothers from destroying the world, or fight them in a war that will probably destroy the world. When he refuses to choose between them, refuses to submit to the binary limitations of a story that he doesn't want, that isn't just or accurate or necessary, that's when Krishna tells him to become himself. *Resist what resists in you*, he says, meaning resist the fear of following a story just because it's an imperfect story. And of course it's an imperfect story. Stories are imperfect because *we* are imperfect beings, and the balcony outside Mr. Henning's window was decorated with intricate wrought iron fretwork.

Through Mr. Henning I met Jo. She was about my age, but more mature, more knowledgeable about how the world worked. Her job was to teach me how to steal, how to bargain, how to survive the world. So I followed her. I was with her when she walked up to the man selling sausages on the corner. She ordered two bratwurst, one for each of us, and once he'd passed us the sausages, wrapped in little buns, we ran, vanished into the crowd, dodging around and disappearing into the chaos of the people and the confusion, and when we found a secluded corner we huddled together, breaking the sausage casings with our teeth and letting the hot grease dribble down our lips. And of course I didn't care about the sausage man, didn't care what he thought, or felt, or any person, man or woman. Because they weren't me. Even if what I was doing was wrong, at least I was in control. So I thought. I was choosing my story, I thought. I'd never been given a story before and now, having found myself in this one, I was hoping it would work.

The Threepenny Opera is a German musical based on a play by John Gay, *The Beggar's Opera*. The hero, Mac the Knife, is an amiable criminal who realizes that all human transactions are basically business transactions, that the only difference between the rich and the poor is: the rich are more skillful at stealing. And by *skillful* I mean they're able to see human beings as insecure, therefore easily manipulated. They take the chaos in the world and use it to make more chaos, a beautiful chaos they try to control, and Jo was showing me how. Like Mac the Knife in *his* story, I was granted, not power, but the freedom to do what I wanted, and although the story was set in motion by Mr. Henning, now it was *mine*, and because it was mine, and because it was elastic, I could shape it. Mack the Knife, by trusting his intuition, meaning the feeling in his gut, meaning the chemical reactions inside his small intestines, instead of following the rules he'd been given, looked around for new rules.

Jo led me to what had once been an outdoor market and now was an open field of bricks and rubble, and around the edges people were pulled into various circles, looking up now and then but furtively, like people in movies when a scene is filmed and you can tell the passersby have been told not to look but they can't help raising their eyes. Jo must have known one circle of people because a boy turned around when she whistled. He looked at me and I could see him gauging me, my age and strength and the euphoria I'd felt a second ago didn't completely dissipate but that's when I thought of my father. He was dying. He was ready to die but it hadn't quite happened, death hadn't happened, and that's the beauty of making up your own story. When Jo put her arm around my shoulder she was indicating that I was acceptable, and space was made for me in the circle and we all started playing a game. One of the boys was chosen to climb up to the top of a rubble hill, and the game was, when he ran down the hill he would try to break through the wall of our bodies, and when he ran down and into our arms, because he didn't break through, he fell to the ground. He was smaller than the others, more my size, and I watched as he curled up in the dirt, not wiggling like a worm because sometimes a worm, if it's scared, doesn't move. And like watching a worm, I waited to see if he would stay where he was, or would he get up. Would he brush off the dust and laugh, and maybe he did laugh, but I was thinking about my father, lying in bed. He'd gotten thin. He was sleeping more and more, eating cans of liquid food and he must've known the end was near, the end of his story, and at some point you have to accept that your story isn't yours. Like the boy in the dirt, curled up. The other boys weren't all blond but when they surrounded him, the game they played was a game of kicking the boy. The first kid stepped up and perfunctorily kicked the boy's leg, which twitched, which seemed to be what they wanted, a reaction. The twitching encouraged others to step up, to aim their shoes at the back of his neck or his chest, and it was how they exorcised their powerlessness, by seeming to hate the boy, but really they hated themselves. And I watched the scene unfold as if I were watching a play, except I had a part in this play, and because apparently we were taking turns, after Jo had given him a kick, that's when she looked at me, not saying a word, as if words were extraneous, as if we'd all been dancing a dance and now it was time for a solo, *my* solo, and the boy must have done something wrong, must have refused to follow a rule, or broken a rule, a made-up rule that let him be part of the group but now he'd failed and whatever he'd done necessitated justice. And it's hard to know what justice is when you're angry, and everyone seemed to be angry. They hadn't started out angry but now they were, and now he was blamed for the world as it was. He was dressed in the same uniform they all were wearing, and Jo was too, her shirt tucked in, her pants rolled up at the ankles. I was the only one wearing shorts, as if I was a child and they were adults and this was my lesson. Or my test. To pass the test I have to be what I never wanted to be, to take my turn in a story that isn't mine, and that's what stories do, they start out going in one direction and then they veer off, and part of being in a story is letting it go, letting the story take you to the place you didn't even know existed but there you are, and yes, there's always a choice, but standing in what had become a circle, the choices I had boiled down to running away or doing what they were asking me to do, not telling me, but it was clear what they wanted. And Friedrich Nietzsche had either syphilis, or bipolar disorder, or somehow a story had infected him. All he had to do was hear the cries of the horse being whipped, and the rest of his story, the running to the horse and embracing the horse, followed from that. Any story, once a trajectory gets started, as the trajectory takes over, the options become fewer and fewer. Every decision becomes the logical continuation of everything that came before, and even if it wasn't logical, once I'd given the boy one kick, the second kick was easier, and the third and fourth seemed to follow, the boy becoming an object, like a bale of hay, or like a vending machine that refuses to cooperate. Kicking it began to feel not good exactly, but a necessary release of everything that was going wrong. For the most part, my mind and body try to act in unison, that's the goal, and to kick the boy I needed my mind to go along with my body. Or at least not get in my way. I had to forget about right and wrong because there was no debating anymore if what I was doing was wrong, I knew it was, and that's what I had to vanquish, the last remnant of my old ideol-ogy, the last vestige of the story I'd been taught, and the only way to do that was to hate the old story, to hate the boy who represented that story, to hate him and punish him and although I knew that ribs can be broken and teeth knocked out, because my mind had ceded responsibility, my body took over. And it wasn't just *my* body. Jo was doing it too, and her friends were, and I'd been allowed to participate. I'd been allowed inside a circle that could be violent, but could also be a circle of safety and support, and like anything new it took some getting used to. Like a lost locust finding a like-minded group, my body got synchronized with them, moving together with them, destroying with them what we had to destroy, proving by our kicking that we were right. It wasn't euphoria but like euphoria, it felt like I'd taken a drug, like I'd placed a pill on my tongue, and I'd like to think that I didn't swallow mine, that I paused, holding the pill between my teeth but the time for pausing had come and gone, and when I looked down at the boy who was looking back at me, his eyes pleading with me, I shut *my* eyes when I kicked him. I thought the kicking would be the end of it, that this was an initiation and once I'd passed the initiation I would be free but instead of being the end, it was only the beginning.

In the beginning is my end. That's T. S. Eliot writing during the Second World War, and by *end* I assume he means not just death but also *What might have been and what has been*, and cyanide was discovered in the 1700s. It's known for a blue color, an almond odor, and because it's supposedly painless it's a popular poison. In 1978, in South America, it was used to kill the members of a settlement in Guyana, a utopian settlement carved out of the jungle by followers of a man named Jim Jones. Jonestown was named for him, and what he led has been called a cult but really it was just a community of people who believed in equality and communality, and most of them were African American, mostly from San Francisco, and most of them accepted their leader's erratic behavior. And like any tyrant with power, he got carried away. The fact that he'd stockpiled cases of cyanide suggests he knew he would get carried away, possibly wanted it, and when his guards, one day, opened fire on a group of people trying to leave his compound, and killed them, because one of them was a United States congressman, Jones saw that his utopia, which had worked for a while, was over. And because he wanted everything *else* to be over, he mixed up a kind of ersatz Kool-Aid, laced it with medications, one of them being cyanide. The beverage was distributed, first to children, then to the mothers and fathers and he was adamant that everyone drink the fruit-flavored concoction. If they believed in him they would be willing to drink, and although some must have hesitated, and some must have realized that what was happening wasn't what they'd signed up for, in the end, hundreds of people swallowed the poison. As did Jones. As did Eva Braun, in Germany, at the end of the war. Along with her new husband, she bit into the small glass vial containing Prussic Acid, a liquid form of cyanide that prevents the absorption of oxygen, and when the cells of the body can't get oxygen, they can't breathe. So they die. And then the body dies. And although it would have been enough to let the almond odor fill his nostrils, to let the pale blue liquid dissolve on his tongue and into his cells, finding its way to the microscopic mechanisms of life, because he wanted to control the narrative of his life, like Eva Braun's husband, Jim Jones shot himself, probably in the head, just to make sure.

My father, when he told me he was ready to die, was propped up in his bed, a white pillow under his neck, a cream-colored blanket tucked around his feet. I remember the hairs in his ears, his watery eyes, and he had what they called hospice care, a nurse who brought drugs. His bed was an electric bed that tilted up, raising his legs or his head and the drugs were on the bedside table, little pills meant to dull his pain, possibly kill it, and killing pain is better than feeling pain but by dulling his senses, or the brain that makes sense of the senses, most of the time he was half asleep. But even half sleeping he was still my father, the person I knew and loved, and love, of course, isn't simple. I'd read about Demeter, the Greek goddess who sacrificed her daughter, Persephone, leaving her in the underworld, a terrible place but a necessary place if spring is to follow from winter. And that's what a story does. It teaches you to believe the story you're in. It convinces you, somehow, that the story will end, and you never know *how* it will end, exactly, but my father, lying in bed, told me he was cold. I knew enough to make him some tea, which I did. I boiled the water, pinched out some dry leaves from the porcelain box we kept above the sink, and when I added the hot water, as the leaves expanded in the cup, as I dug the last of the sugar out of the glass jar, I had an inkling that the story I was in had somehow gone off course. There I was, like Edmund, using my finger to stir the sugar into the tea, tasting the tea to make sure it was sweet, and like Edmund I found myself carrying the cup to my father's bed. I'm proud of you, he said, proud of the person you've become, proud of the things you've done and will do, and like me, Edmund had tasted the bitterness of the tea, but the sugar made it bearable, *it* being the poison he'd added, if it *was* poison, and it was, and it's warm, his father said, holding the cup with both hands, and because he was cold he drank it.

In all the versions of *The Threepenny Opera*, at the end of the story, the narrative suddenly changes course. Mack the Knife, having been arrested for his crimes and locked in a gaol, awaits his execution. *Crime never pays.* That's the story we've all been told but *The Threepenny Opera*, by acknowledging the fungibility of *all* stories, changes the narrative. Mackie is allowed to go free. A god-like machine releases him into the world where he marries his girl. He loves her and marries her, and I assume he lives happily after the story is over, but Edmund's story isn't quite over. You see him walking along a bombed-out street, eyes cast down, watching the paving stones as he steps from one to the other, not meeting anyone's eyes because he's watching his feet, step after step, moving but without destination, not technically lost because there's nowhere he's going, randomly walking under the gray sky, and random seems reasonable, as good a direction as any he's tried, and after walking in circles all afternoon, at a certain point he notices, as he passes a doorway he's probably passed before, standing in the shadows of the doorway, a man and a woman embracing. Nothing unusual in that. The man wears a uniform and the woman is young, and whether she looks like Jo, or whether she *is* Jo, Edmund stands on the cobblestones waiting for her to look up and see him. And because she doesn't look up he assumes she didn't hear him call her name. And then, when she does look up, although no door is hanging in the place where a door would have been, because she gives no sign of recognition, no acknowledgement in her eyes or arms that Edmund even exists, when she turns away it's like she's closing the door, an invisible door but once it's shut, although he doesn't know what it means, he feels what it means. Whatever story he'd tried to make his own, whatever story might have freed him from the story he couldn't seem to escape from, because he didn't escape . . . By the time you get to that point you really *are* between two worlds, floating almost as you walk between buildings, feeling the eyes of people watching not *you* but a version of you, not a camera, barely human, more like a shell, a dead shell, and even brainless animals emerge from their shells. They live and they die and I'm not thinking about dying because I'm still trying to learn how to live, pretending to live by telling my story again and again in the hope that something might change, that some coincidence might give me control or a sense of control, and it's not a coincidence when, having wandered into a ruined building, I find a stick. It's the same stick I always seem to find, and I know what to do with it. I mark out some hopscotch squares in the dirt. In the story I start hopping from square to square, following the rules of the game, trying to maintain some order, or create some order and I also use the stick to tap loose plaster off the walls. The stick is perfect for that. So that's what I do, walking up the crumbling stairs, touching the tip of my stick to the bricks and beams, and the stick can also be a sword. And a sword is perfect for fighting, *against* something or *for* something, and either way, when I climb to the top of the building I imagine the stick becoming a spear, and like pictures I've seen of javelin throwers I throw it, over the side of the building. In the story I watch it float, not like a feather but it's light, and it sails slowly down to the street below. In the story the street was filled with people, moving around like people busy with errands and appointments, but now the street is empty. In the story I must have been dizzy, or lightheaded, or maybe I stepped on a loose piece of brick and lost my balance. Probably I jump

References

Aeschylus. *The Oresteia [Agamemnon, Libation Bearers, Eumenides]* c. 500 BCE, Athens.

Bacon, Francis. *Study after Velasquez's Portrait of Pope Innocent X* (1953). Oil on canvas. Des Moines Art Center, Des Moines.

—. *Triptych, May—June 1973* (1973). Private Collection, Switzerland.

Picasso, Pablo. *Las Meninas* (1957). Oil on canvas. Museu Picasso, Barcelona.

Velasquez, Diego. *Pope Innocent X* (c. 1650). Oil on canvas. Doria Pamphilj Gallery, Rome.

—. *Las Meninas* (1656). Oil on canvas. Prado Museum, Madrid.

***

Alexander, F. Matthias. *Man's Supreme Inheritance*. London: Mouritz, 1996.

—. *The Use of the Self*, London: Methuen, 1932.

Antonioni, Michelangelo, dir. *Blow-Up*. Carlo Ponti Productions, 1966. 111 min.

Birkin, Jane & Gainsbourg, Serge. *Je t'aime . . . moi non plus*. Fontana Records. 1969.

Bond, Edward. *Lear*. Premiered 1971, London, The Royal Court Theater.

—. *Lear*. London: Eyre Methuen, 1972.

—. *Saved*. London: Eyre Methuen, 1973.

Cortázar, Julio. *Blow-Up: And Other Stories*. Translated by Paul Blackburn. New York: Pantheon, 1985.

Gelb, Michael. *Body Learning: An Introduction to the Alexander Technique*. New York: Henry Holt and Co., 1981.

***

Allen, James, ed. *Without Sanctuary: Lynching Photography in America*. Los Angeles: Twin Palms, 1999.

Brecht, Bertolt. *The Collected Poems*. New York: Liveright, 2018.

Gardner, Alexander. *Execution of the Conspirators*. Gelatin silver print. 1865.

McGuire, Barry, performer. *Eve of Destruction*. Hullabaloo, NBC. 1965.

Meinhof, Ulrike. *Everybody Talks About the Weather . . . We Don't*. Translated by Louise Von Flotow. New York: Seven Stories Press, 2008.

Penn, Arthur, dir. *Bonnie and Clyde*, Warner Bros. 1967. 111 min.

Richter, Gerhard. *October 18, 1977* (1988). Oil on canvas. New York, MOMA.

Sloan, P.F., writer. *Eve of Destruction*. Dunhill Records. 1965.

***

Rainer, Yvonne, *Trio A*. Premiered 1966, New York, Judson Memorial Church.

—. *Trio A (The Mind Is a Muscle, Part 1)* Recorded 1978, 10:30 min.

—. *Feelings are Facts: a Life*. 2006. MIT Press.

Brown, Trisha. *Accumulation*. New York. 1971.

—. *Man Walking Down the Side of a Building*. New York. 1970.

—. *Roof Piece*. New York. 1971.

Cage, John. *Water Walk*. 1959 (Performed 1960, *I've Got a Secret*. CBS Television).

Forti, Simone. *See Saw*. Reuben Gallery, (Robert McElroy, photographer) New York. 1960.

Sontag, Susan. *On Photography*. (1977) London: Penguin. (Arbus pages 32–48).

—. *Against Interpretation*. (1966) New York: FSG.

***

Brecht, Bertolt. *Der gute Mensch von Sezuan*. Premiered 1943,

Zürich Schauspielhaus.

—. *The Good Person of Szechwan*. Translated by John Willet. London: Bloomsbury. 2015.

Frank, Melvin, dir. *The Court Jester*. 1955. 101 min.

Kaye, Danny. *The Danny Kaye Show*. (Oct. 23, 1963). Season 1, Episode 5, featuring Gene Kelly. CBS.

Reifenstahl, Leni, dir. *Triumph of the Will* (*Triumph des Willens*) 1935. 114 min.

Truffaut, François. *Hitchcock/Truffaut*. New York: Simon & Schuster, 1983.

Wagner, Richard. *Die Meistersinger von Nürnberg*. Premiered 1868, Munich, National Theater.

***

Naruse, Mikio, dir. *When a Woman Ascends the Stairs*, Toho. 1960, 101 min.

***

Abbot of Eynsham. *Aelfric's Lives of Saints*. London. 1881.

Botticelli, Sandro. *The Cestello Annunciation*. (c. 1489) Tempera on wood. Uffizi Gallery, Florence.

Dryer, Carl Theodor, dir. *The Passion of Joan of Arc*, 1928.

Gentileschi, Artemisia. *Annunciation*. (1630) Oil on Panel. Museo di Capodimonte, Naples.

Ginsberg, Allen, *Untitled (Mock Machete Battle)*. Gelatin silver print. 1954.

Giorgi, Rosa. *Saints in Art*. Los Angeles: J. Paul Getty Museum, 2003.

Haskell, Barbara. *Agnes Martin*. New York: Whitney Museum of American Art, 1992.

Keats, John. *Endymion*. London: Taylor and Hessey, 1818.

Moore, Marianne. *Complete Poems*. New York. Penguin, 1994.

Steiglitz, Alfred. *Georgia O'Keeffe*. New York: Metropolitan Museum of Art, 1978.

***

Alighieri, Dante. *Divine Comedy (Inferno, Purgatorio, Paradiso)*. c. 1308–1321.

Dassin, Jules, dir. *Phaedra* (from Euripides' *Hippolytus*) 1962. 115 min.

Hitchcock, Alfred, dir. *Psycho*, 1960, 109 min.

Litvak, Anatole, dir. *Five Miles to Midnight* (*Le Couteau dans la plaie*), 1962. 110 min.

Mann, Delbert, dir. *Desire Under the Elms*, 1958, 111 min.

O'Neill, Eugene. *Desire Under the Elms*, Premiered 1924, New York, Provincetown Playhouse.

Welles, Orson, dir. *The Trial* (from Franz Kafka's *The Trial*), 1962. 118 min.

***

Brecht, Bertolt. *The Threepenny Opera*, Premiered 1928, Berlin, Theater am Schiffbauerdamm.

Brook, Peter, and Carriere, Jean-Claude. *The Mahabharata*, London: Metheun, 1985.

Eliot, T. S. *Four Quartets*. New York: Harcourt, Brace and Company, 1943.

Rosellini, Roberto, dir. *Germany, Year Zero*, 1948, 78 min.

Acknowledgments

I am grateful to the various writers who have touched my life, including...

Marcelle Clements, Richard Nelson, Brigid Hughes, Hilton Als, Arthur Danto, Robyn Schiff, Geoff Dyer, Maggie Nelson, Ben Kunkel, Betsy Sussler, Frederic Tuten, Garielle Lutz, Annie-B Parson, August Wilson, Francine Prose, Ben Marcus, Dana Spiotta, Wallace Shawn, Jonathan Lethem, Carl Watson, Lydia Davis, Blake Tewksbury, Leanne Shapton, Colson Whitehead, Leigh Newman, Lance Olsen, Meghan Daum, Forrest Gander, Paul Lafarge, Mary Beth Hughes, James Hannaham, Miranda July, Wells Tower, Ed Park, Anelise Chen, James Kelman, Jonathan Dee, Allen Ginsberg, Valeria Luiselli, Paul Muldoon, Blake Butler, Eleni Sikelianos, Edward Bond, Jim Crace, Mandy Jacobson David Salle, Alix Lambert, Sigrid Nunez, Desmond Barry, Heidi Julavitz, Victor LaValle, Catherine Foulkrod, Antoine Wilson, Wayne Koestenbaum, John Jeremiah Sullivan, Évita Yumul, George Trow, Andrew Sean Greer, Brian Blanchfield, David Mamet, Peter Brook, Rachel Khong, Andrew Sarris, Rivka Galchen, Eugene Lim, Amina Cain, Meghan O'Rourke, Donald Antrim, Patti Smith, John Dermot Woods, Fiona Maazel, Joshua Furst, Patrick Deville, Terese Svoboda, Greg Gerke, Charles Simic, Daphne Kolotay, John Wray, Manuel Martinez, Nam Le, Yiyun Li, Peter Zilahy, Suzanne Dottino, Nick Flynn, A.M. Homes, Brett Fletcher Lauer, Ander Monson, Heather Cleary, Joshua Ferris, Laurie Weeks, Anna Moschovakis, Spalding Gray, Antonia Logue, Ben Lerner, Pejk Malinovski, Lewis Hyde, Peter Cameron, Lynn Tillman, Jonathan Ames, Tao Lin, Mandy Jacobson, John P. Shanley, Giancarlo DiTrapano, James Yeh, Harriet Haskell...

Author's Note

A book takes time. Writing, printing, reading, thinking are part of a slow technology. And sharing is also part of that process. If you liked this book, and even if you didn't, tell someone, pass it on, give it or loan it or use it to begin a conversation